A VISCOUNT FOR VIOLET

THE BLOOMING BRIDES BOOK 4

ELLIE ST. CLAIR

Facebook: Ellie St. Clair

Cover by AJF Designs

Do you love historical romance? Receive access to a free ebook, as well as exclusive content such as giveaways, contests, freebies and advance notice of pre-orders through my mailing list!

Sign up here!

Also By Ellie St. Clair

Blooming Brides
A Duke for Daisy
A Marquess for Marigold
An Earl for Iris
A Viscount for Violet

The Blooming Brides Box Set: Books 1-4

For a full list of all of Ellie's books, please see
www.elliestclair.com/books.

1

Violet closed her eyes and sighed in contentment. There was nothing quite like the thrill of antici- pation when beginning a new story.

Finally. She had spent the morning determined to finish her household tasks as quickly as possible so she could sneak away to spend at least an hour here, in one of her quiet places. She opened the book in front of her, inhaling the scent of the ink upon the crisp pages.

She had visited the small book section of the general store just yesterday. She had convinced her father to part with a few coins, emphasizing the need to bolster the shelves of the sitting room in the family's inn. Her father had reluctantly agreed after Violet demonstrated the number of boarders who frequented the room and perused the shelves for something in which they might be interested. She had been sure to pick up a few volumes recounting historic battles or exploits of various explorers, but she had also snuck in a gothic novel and a book of sonnets to add to her collection.

She opened the novel now with a swirl of emotions.

On the one hand, there was seldom a romance she didn't enjoy. On the other...

She wasn't sure if it was the marriages of her sisters or her own recent misplaced emotions and attraction, but Violet was beginning to despair that the closest she might ever come to finding true love herself would be through the heroines in the pages of her books.

For one thing, she was likely never going to leave this sleepy town, as much as she loved it, and for another, the boarders who arrived here hardly even acknowledged her existence, besides the fact that she put food in front of them and cleaned their rooms.

She sighed. She was being as dramatic as her sister Iris. Back to her book.

Violet tucked a piece of hair behind her ear and leaned back into the cushion she had placed on the bench in the corner of the garden behind the inn. If there was one thing her mother paid attention to, it was her flowerbeds, and Violet certainly reaped the benefits of it. She was the only one who ever seemed to spend any time in here, besides her mother, and she loved the colors of the blooms and the scent of the sea that continually hung in the air around the inn.

She set the book on her knees, but just as she began to read, a voice filled her ears — one she had been listening to her entire life and at this moment in time, she would dearly love to ignore.

"Violet! Violet, where are you? Oh, I know you are in here, I saw you enter the gardens. Don't pretend you can't hear me."

Maybe if she ignored her long enough, Iris would truly believe she was elsewhere. But no. In moments, her sister was standing in front of her, hands planted on her hips, though Violet kept her eyes on her book.

"Violet, I know you would much rather read than listen to anything I have to say, but this is good news," Iris said, and Violet finally lifted her eyes to her sister, who stood there looking as vivacious as ever, a lavender dress draped over her generous curves, a smile on her red lips.

"Yes?"

"Daisy has arrived!"

"Oh, wonderful!" Violet exclaimed, true joy filling her. All three of her sisters had married in the past year. Daisy spent most of her time with her husband in London, Marigold at her husband's estate in the relatively close Cambridge. Iris and her husband were living at the inn as he remained in hiding, for his identity was known to the French, on whom he had spied.

"No need to rise, Vi," she heard Daisy say, and Violet ignored her and surged to her feet. "We shall come to you."

"Oh, Daisy, I am so glad to see you!" Violet said, rushing into the arms of her eldest sister, seeing Marigold trailing along behind. Her stomach was still flat, but Violet could practically see the look of joy on Marigold's face as she had just found out she was expecting. "It seems like it has been so long."

"It has, hasn't it?" Daisy asked. Then she waved a hand to the other nearby benches. "Shall we sit for a moment?"

"Of course," Violet said, putting her book down underneath her, unable to ignore the slightest tinge of regret that she hadn't had time to begin it. Later, she promised herself as Marigold's dog, Clover, raced into the garden and brushed against her feet. "Tell us of London and all of your magnificent estates."

And so they did. Violet hoped they wouldn't ask of all that had recently occurred at the inn, but Daisy had questions.

"I hear there was quite a bit of excitement recently," she said, and Iris and Violet exchanged a look before Iris nodded.

"I suppose it is to be expected when the inn continues to welcome men recently returned from war," Iris said before beginning her retelling. She dragged out the story much longer than necessary, but Violet was grateful she left out some of the details.

"I don't understand," Daisy said. "How did the French spy, Comtois, know so much about Iris' husband, Lord Westwood?"

"I suppose because he was a spy," Iris said after an awkward pause. "That is what he does."

"That is not it at all," Violet countered, unable to look at her sisters. "It was because I told him."

"You what?" Daisy asked.

"He flirted with me a bit, and I stupidly fell for his charms," Violet said, biting her lip. Iris and Marigold already knew the particulars, having been there, and Violet was loath to revisit her stupidity. But she wouldn't lie.

"It wasn't your fault, Vi," Marigold said with a gentle hand on her arm. "Any of us would have fallen for him."

"Iris didn't," she said. "She saw through him the entire time."

"Yes, well, I have a sense for that kind of thing," Iris said, but Violet shook her head.

"And I clearly have none."

"That is certainly not the case," Marigold countered, but

Violet was well aware that her soft-hearted sister was simply trying to console her.

"Marigold—"

"Girls? Where are you?"

"It's Mother," Daisy said. "We'd best be going in."

"Time to make dinner, I suppose," Violet said with a sigh. She'd thought she had carved out a bit of time for herself, but with the arrival of Daisy and Marigold and their husbands, there would likely be much more work to do.

"Actually, Mother said that tonight we would have the new maids see to dinner," Iris said with a triumphant grin, and Violet looked at her incredulously.

"Are you sure about that?"

"I am," she said. "Perhaps our parents are beginning to realize that the four of us will not be here to run the inn forever."

Violet bit her lip but said nothing as the sisters began for the house.

"Here," Daisy said, placing a hand on Violet's arm. "You nearly forgot this."

She put the book into her hand, giving Violet's fingers a little squeeze as she passed it over. "I'm sorry we interrupted you," she added with a smile, and Violet shook her head.

"I would much rather spend time with you," she reassured her as they filed into the sitting room where their parents awaited.

"Oh, how wonderful it is to have you all home together once more!" their mother, Alice, said once they had settled themselves on the rather worn grouping of furniture. The room would have otherwise been rather drab, but for the bouquets her mother had brought in from the garden and placed in vases on some of the mismatched end tables. "And I hope your husbands will join us soon. We have much to discuss with them, but first, we'd like to speak to the four of you."

The sisters nodded, looking at one in another with some question in their eyes. This was rather odd. Their parents were typically out of the ordinary, but this seemed more out of character than usual.

"You know that we have relied on the four of you to do much of the work around here."

Iris snorted, and while Daisy stared at her with a warning glare, for once Violet agreed with Iris. Their parents would have been out of business years ago if it wasn't for her and her sisters.

"Yes, Father," Marigold said, always the one attempting peace.

"Well, with three of you married now — Iris, I know you are still here, but you will be leaving eventually — we've had to think of what we might do with the inn. We would like to stay here for a while at least but... it may prove difficult, financially. Which is why our solution is so perfect."

"You are going to sell the inn?" Violet cried, then brought a hand to her mouth to stem any further protest. Why should it bother her in the least if that was the choice they made? It wasn't as though she particularly enjoyed any of the tasks she undertook here. It was interesting that the thought should bring her melancholy instead of joy. She supposed it was because the inn was home. It was where she had grown up and was all she knew. If they didn't have the inn — if *she* didn't have the inn — then what did she have? What would she do with her life?

"I'm not sure if *sell* is the right word," her mother began, but then their father chimed in and got right to the point, as he always did.

"While we have certainly been blessed by the four of

6

you, we also realize that we cannot gift the inn to any of our daughters," he said, though Violet would have countered that point. Why couldn't they? "Having no son, I was never sure what our plan would be. But as you know, my good friend George Anderson's sons have always felt like my own."

Violet wasn't entirely sure of that either. She had met them a few times throughout her life, but the Anderson family lived quite a distance away in Leicester, which wasn't exactly conducive to much time spent together.

"His eldest is going to follow in his footsteps running George's inn, but his second son is also interested in staying involved in the business. George wrote to me with a proposal."

He chuckled, and Violet shared looks with her sisters, as they were not entirely sure what was humorous about the situation.

"Linus is not only looking for an inn of his own, but he is also looking for a bride."

Oh, dear. Now her father's chuckle made a little more sense.

"I would be happy to have him take over our Wild Rose Inn, but I would also like to keep the inn within the family. There seems to be quite an easy solution to all of this. Violet," he looked over at her. "I wouldn't agree to this without your acceptance, but this may be perfect. You could stay in Southwold, marry Linus, and you would never have to leave the inn you love so much. What do you say?"

All eyes turned to Violet, who sat on the edge of the ugly floral-printed sofa, stunned at her father's request. Why he thought she so loved the inn, she had no idea, and what did it say that he didn't think her capable of finding a husband on her own? It wasn't as though she had been searching long. She had only recently come of the age when it would be prudent to begin considering marriage. Why, Daisy had been five years older than Violet's current age when she finally married.

"I, ah... I'm not entirely sure," she said slowly, and of course, Iris had something to say about the situation even if Daisy did not.

"Oh, Father, you cannot ask Violet to do such a thing. Why, we haven't even seen Linus for at least ten years. He was terrible as a child. He could be a beast for all we know! How do you know Violet even wants to stay here? You know she has always wanted to see the world beyond Southwold. And besides all of that, this is ridiculous. You are simply *giving* away the inn?"

Their father colored and looked down.

"Well..." he muttered. "As it happens, I do owe George some money, so he suggested this was one way to forgive all of that."

"You borrowed money from him? And now you're going to sell off Violet in return?" Iris asked, her cheeks turning ashen, reflecting all that Violet was currently feeling inside.

"I was not asking what you thought of this, Iris," her father said with more ire than he usually portrayed, and they all simply stared at him in surprise.

Violet took a breath.

"Iris does have a point, Father," she said. "Though I now understand why you have asked this of me. Perhaps... perhaps I could spend some time with Linus and determine then if I would be willing to marry him?"

She was well aware that she might never find a husband otherwise. Would it be better to be married to a man she hardly knew, than to never marry at all?

That remained to be seen.

2

Owen Ridlington watched the four women file into the house from the garden. It was interesting how they could all be similar yet also quite unique individuals. He had been aware of this family for some time — since the Crown had first been looking for a place such as this, where soldiers and the like could convalesce or hide as the case may be. The owner, Elias Tavners, had been more than accepting of the idea, a former soldier himself and one who clearly longed for days gone by.

They had never expected that the inn would be compromised.

August Williams, the Earl of Westwood, had inadvertently changed that.

"Lovely women, are they not?"

Speak of the devil. Owen had sensed the man approaching behind him but had hoped if he ignored him, he would leave him be for the moment. Lord Westwood wasn't a bad sort. He was good company, could tell quite a tale, and was welcoming of all. He was just somewhat... inept.

"They seem to be," he agreed, and Lord Westwood chuckled.

"I have no issue with you saying so of my wife, if that is what you are concerned about," he said, but Owen shook his head at the mention of Iris.

"Not at all," he said. "I have a job to do here, and no time to be watching the women pass by."

"Your job — to watch over me."

"Which has now extended to all who are here at the inn," Owen added. "Those who followed you may have told others of your whereabouts. The inn could be in jeopardy now."

Lord Westwood had been a spy within the French courts. He had not ascertained much, but it seemed someone had discovered his identity. He was pulled out of France to this inn in Southwold but nonetheless, he was found. There were currently British operatives who were attempting to determine if the secret was safe or not, and Owen could hardly wait for the day they could both take their leave. It wasn't that he didn't like Southwold or The Wild Rose Inn. He was simply bored.

"I know what you are thinking," Westwood said, and Owen looked over at him, hoping the man did not. "That if I had been a better spy, you wouldn't be here right now."

"That's not it at all," Owen countered, though it most certainly was. "I simply am looking forward to returning home when the time comes, that is all."

"And to you, home is...?"

"Sheffield. And London," Owen said, and Westwood tilted his head to look at him.

"What do you do there?"

Owen paused. He preferred to be known for what he did within the war effort rather than outside of it.

"I look after the needs of the people and the land."

"Are you a steward?"

"No."

"Do you work for a nobleman?"

"No."

"Are you a landowner?"

"Yes."

"I never knew such a thing," Westwood said with some surprise. "How did you come by such land?"

"It's entailed."

"Entailed? Then you must be—"

"Titled. Yes. Lord Primrose."

"No."

Owen chuckled at Westwood's astonished look.

"I am a viscount. Not a particularly attendant one. Hence, my role here."

Westwood looked aghast.

"Your exploits are legendary as Owen Ridlington, and yet I have never heard mention of a Lord Primrose. How can that be?"

"Because I did not wish my true identity to be known within the military," Owen said with a shrug. "I'd rather be known for what I do than what I was born into. To be rewarded with a position rather than given one simply because of who I am."

"Fair point," Westwood said, walking over to the side table and pouring drinks for the two of them. "Here you are, Ridling— Primrose. I hardly know if I can look at you the same anymore."

"I would ask that you do. And that you keep this secret better than you ever uncovered one. I'd rather others not be aware. I far prefer to stay in the shadows, as it were. Makes it easier to look after everyone else."

"Fair enough, *Ridlington*," Westwood said before taking a sip of his drink. "Who looks after your estates, then, while you are keeping England safe?"

"I have an estate manager and only one estate," he said with a shrug. "My father was not particularly prudent, and when he passed, he left debts that required the selling off of some properties — anything that was not entailed. It makes things easier, at any rate, for I prefer keeping busy with more than a pen and paper."

"How very... fortunate," Westwood said, though he raised an eyebrow while he did, clearly displaying how he would have felt were he left behind such a situation.

"You could say that," Owen said with a shrug. "I know most noblemen would despair of such a state, but to be honest, Westwood, if I wasn't taking part in the war effort, I would be much happier spending my days on the grounds of my estates, working with the horses and the harvest with my own hands rather than from behind a desk or through correspondence. It's what I'll likely go back to someday."

"What about the Season?" Westwood asked. "You have no desire to spend any time in London?"

"None at all," Owen said with a bit of a laugh. "If I had a choice, I would give the title away."

Westwood shook his head.

"Well, we are glad to have you here among us for now, that is for certain," he said. "I feel a mite safer with the man who is known for taking down French spies and protecting the Prince Regent himself when needed."

"I cannot recall ever admitting to such," Owen said with a frown. While he wasn't a spy, most of his work had been done without even those he was protecting being aware of his accomplishments.

"You don't have to," Westwood said, "And I'll keep your

secret if it matters so much to you. At any rate, I'd best be finding my wife. Good day to you, Ridlington."

Owen tipped his hat to him, crossed his arms, and leaned back against the windowsill, content, for the moment, to enjoy the view beyond.

~

"I SIMPLY DO NOT THINK you should agree to it, Violet," Iris said as she helped Violet prepare the table outdoors. Since Violet's three sisters had all married gentlemen of the nobility — former military men, all three — her mother and father were attempting their utmost to entertain as they assumed the men were used to, despite the gentlemen's protests.

"A picnic outdoors," her mother had said earlier that morning, "is just the thing! Why, all the *ton* do so."

"I understand that we might enjoy it, Mother," Marigold had said diplomatically. "But I do not think it is necessary in order to please our husbands."

"Nonsense!" Alice had exclaimed. "Now, Violet, you will prepare everything, will you not?"

And so Violet did, though her sisters were kind enough to help. Why, even Daisy and Marigold went down to the kitchens to help collect everything that some of the new staff had prepared.

This was one idea of her mother's, however, that Violet didn't overly mind. While she wasn't often found traipsing through the woods or marshes as Marigold had always been wont to do, she did love being outdoors, in the family's gardens or in one of the comfortable spots that could be found along the seashore. She was usually with a book in hand, but she still felt that she was enjoying nature, in her own way.

She thought that perhaps she might enjoy setting the table more than actually eating with her family, though she would have to do so regardless. Each dinner since her sisters' return to visit was something of a nightmare as her father attempted to impress the three gentlemen at his table with his own stories of his war efforts, though they all humored him well enough.

She came back to the present moment when she felt Iris staring at her, waiting for a response.

"What was that?" Violet asked.

"I said," Iris began, clearly attempting patience as she placed her hands on her hips, "that I do not think you should agree to this ridiculous idea of Father's."

"Well, I clearly have no good judgment of my own," Violet said with a shrug, attempting nonchalance despite how painful it was to speak of. "So why not do as Father asks? What else I am to do with my life?"

"What do you *want* to do?" Iris asked, and Violet sighed.

"I am not entirely sure," she said as she turned from Iris to continue her table setting. "In my novels, it seems that everything happens as the heroine would like it to happen, even if she doesn't know what that will be until later. I read one recently in which the young woman is sent to a seaside resort town because she is deemed nearly mad by her father — though not mad enough to be sent to an asylum. She actually enjoys it there, but, of course, has no idea what direction her life might take, for the town is composed of mostly women. Then one day, a group of men come to town because they are looking for somewhere to train for war. So she meets one of the men, and they end up falling in love. He, of course, is a duke — kind of like Daisy's life, isn't it? — and she is whisked away. She is then able to greet her father once more and allow him to see how she is now incredibly happy and powerful and that he was in the wrong about who she was. She wasn't mad, she simply had ideas other than his own. You should read it."

"I should, should I?"

Violet gasped at the masculine voice behind her, and she whirled in its direction, startled to find she was alone with one of their boarders — Owen Ridlington, the soldier who was sent to protect Lord Westwood.

"Mr. Ridlington!" she said, a hand — still holding a plate — at her breast. "Where did you— what did you— where is Iris?"

"Your sister left a few moments ago. To where, I have no idea," he drawled in that slow, leisurely manner of his. "You seemed quite animated as you recounted your story, and I didn't want to interrupt. Besides, it sounded so interesting that I thought even I might give it a try, though you've spoiled the ending for me now."

Warmth rushed to Violet's cheeks. Surely if she touched her face her hands would come away scorched.

"Yes, well, if you'd like, it is on the shelves in your sitting room," she said, unable to meet his eyes.

Violet had a difficult time speaking with any good-looking man, which Mr. Ridlington was, in a somewhat... mysterious way. He was tall, with a lanky build, and unlike some of the others around here — particularly her own sisters' husbands — he dressed quite casually in simple trousers and a linen shirt. He kept a pistol tucked into the waistband of his pants and usually wore a hat — which was rather short with a long brim in the back — so low over his eyes that it was difficult to see his face. She would have hardly known what he looked like had he not had to remove it for mealtimes, for his chin and the lower half of his cheeks was covered with a beard as dark as the hair upon his head.

"I thank you for the recommendation," he said, and Violet wondered if she was hearing things, or if that was laughter in his voice. "An interesting idea, setting a table outdoors."

"My mother would like our family to have a picnic for lunch this afternoon," she said, resuming her task so she would no longer have to look at him. "She feels that this would be of interest to the gentlemen."

Mr. Ridlington chuckled lowly, something about it stirring Violet deep within, but she ignored the sensation. This man made her uncomfortable, though most of it was not his own doing, but the fact that he had witnessed Violet at her worst, during a moment of complete embarrassment.

"Somehow I do not think the gentlemen have much of a care whether they eat within your mother's garden or in a dining room," he said. "Picnics are more for women."

"I cannot say I have any particular knowledge on the subject," she said, though she had read of a picnic in one story. It hadn't ended well, as in that story the dogs had come running out of the house and had eaten all of the food. The guests had been quite upset. She didn't think they would have to worry about that today as there was only the well-behaved Clover, Marigold's dog.

"Neither do I," he mused, though she hadn't asked. "If I am eating out of doors, it is typically alone with a meal from the saddlebag."

She smiled at the thought, though she wasn't entirely sure how to respond.

"Do you need a hand?" he asked, and Violet hurriedly shook her head.

"Oh, of course not," she said, finally looking up and

meeting his eyes. They were a warm brown with flecks of gold that she could see from the distance between them, as he stood slouched against a tree. "I'm almost done. And I'm sure Iris will return any moment."

"I'm sure she will," he said, though with the slightest hint of a smile that told Violet Mr. Ridlington was no fool and knew as well as she that there was little chance of Iris returning. "Good day to you, then, Miss Violet," he said as he pushed off the tree and began walking away.

"Good day," Violet replied as she returned to her task, though now with a slight bit of unease that she just couldn't describe.

3

Owen entered the inn just as Alice Tavners was flitting through the foyer. He smiled at her in greeting and moved to continue on his way.

"Oh, Mr. Ridlington!" she called as he passed by, and he turned around to see her waving him back toward her.

"Yes, Mrs. Tavners?"

"I have a favor to ask of you."

Owen sighed, as he had a feeling this would not be one which would be a pleasure to help with.

"Of course, Mrs. Tavners."

"Well, you see, I have a bit of a conundrum as it were. We are to have a picnic in the garden this afternoon with the family. I thought it would be quite what the gentlemen are used to, you see. However, the issue is with this particular plight."

"Hmmm," was all he said in response, waiting for her to continue, as he was not at all sure how he could help her with table settings and she seemed to be talking in circles.

"I have one daughter who is, at the moment, unattached. It makes our table quite lopsided. As I was reviewing everything, I came to the conclusion that we should likely fill the place so that it does not seem so awkward."

He finally realized where she might be going with this, but he waited for her to continue.

"Well," she continued when he didn't make an offer, "I was hoping that, perhaps, you might fill the final seat at our table for today. You have been here for some time, and we know that we can trust you. You are also close with our Lord Westwood."

If by close she meant that he had helped save the man's life, then very well, close they were.

"Thank you for the offer, Mrs. Tavners, but that won't be necessary," he said. "I'm sure your family wouldn't want an outsider in their midst."

"Oh, of course they would love to have you there!" she exclaimed. "Besides, you are not an outsider at all, having lived with us for so long. Also, I'm sure Mr. Tavners would be happy to have another man there who was not so... titled, if you understand what I am saying."

He had a feeling he did. He smiled, though Mrs. Tavners couldn't know what he was thinking — that he was just like the rest of the gentlemen she despaired of her husband looking a fool in front of.

Well, it was not as though he had anything else to do this afternoon, and perhaps the lunch could be somewhat entertaining.

"Very well, Mrs. Tavners, I would be happy to join you," he said. "Thank you for the invitation."

"Oh, good!" she said, clearly relieved. "We shall begin in an hour. See you shortly."

He nodded, then placed his hands on his hips as he watched her walk away. For a woman whose head was always in the clouds, her daughters seemed particularly sensible. One thing was for certain — this would be one of the more interesting engagements of which he had been a part.

~

THE FAMILY'S heads swiveled toward him in surprise when he joined them in the gardens a short time later. He nodded at them in turn as Alice Tavners hastily explained that she had, in fact, invited him. He smiled at Violet, the youngest and the one he had come upon in the gardens that afternoon, as he took a seat beside her.

His smile became slightly broader as he remembered the spirited accounting of her book. Since he had arrived, he had hardly heard her speak any more than what had been necessary. She was a willowy thing, and at first glance, she seemed somewhat meek. He had seen firsthand, however, that she had a bit more spunk than others might give her credit for. When her sister had been in danger, she hadn't hesitated to do all she could.

She had certainly displayed passion as she recounted her tale earlier. He hadn't intended to embarrass her, but it seemed he had nonetheless. Her cheeks had flushed a bright pink from both her enthusiasm as well as the fact that he had caught her speaking to herself. He had just been passing through to the house when he had seen Iris' attention caught by her husband, and she had left her sister in the gardens on her own.

Owen also hadn't been able to help but notice what a pretty thing Violet was. Even now, the sun glinted off of the gold that shone through the darker pieces of her hair, as she left her head unadorned. When she shyly returned his smile, he froze for a moment as her eyes bore into him. He hadn't realized before just how vivid they were. He had never seen anything quite like it — eyes the color of violets in the spring. Hence, her name. Obviously.

He cleared his throat when he realized the table had quieted as they looked at him. He wasn't typically one to make much of a speech, particularly in front of such a crowd, so he simply smiled, removed his hat, and said, "Thank you."

"Yes, well, we are very glad to have you, Mr. Ridlington, are we not?" Alice said before looking beseechingly at her husband. It was her eldest daughter, however, who came to her rescue.

"We are all very fortunate to be here today," Daisy said, and the rest of them quickly agreed before one of the maids came from the inn to begin serving them.

"Who is attending to the rest of our guests?" Elias asked, and Violet answered quietly, "They have already eaten, Father," which seemed to appease him. Interesting that the man hardly knew what was happening within the inn that he apparently owned and managed.

"What do you say after our luncheon is over we men head inside for a game of chance?" Elias continued, and the rest of the family looked down at their plates, leading Owen to suspect that this was a regular occurrence.

"Another time, Elias," said Daisy's husband, the Duke of Greenwich. "Daisy and I were going to go for a walk this afternoon."

"Oh, to your mysterious hiding place, Daisy?" Iris asked with a smirk. "What will you do there?"

"Iris!" Marigold admonished under her breath, but Owen heard it nonetheless. He would have liked to chuckle but knew that might not be the best response at this moment.

"This is a beautiful place for a luncheon," Daisy said, ignoring her sister in a clear attempt at polite conversation, and Owen could see that despite her humble upbringing, she had a countenance befitting of a duchess. "I don't think I ever appreciated this garden the way I should have. Not like you do, Vi."

"None of us did," Marigold said, and Violet lifted a delicate shoulder in response.

"She mostly reads here," Iris said. "It's somewhere quiet, where no one can find you to add to your duties, isn't that right, Vi?"

"Not entirely," she said, looking at her sister pointedly. "It is quiet, but I simply enjoy the surroundings out here, that is all."

"Which is why I have made sure that you will be able to continue to do so," Elias said with a wide grin, and Owen was confused when Violet looked up at her father, shaking her head.

"We believe we are going to be leaving the inn," Elias said to Owen, taking him aback. "We have an interested family friend — a man just like a son, really — and he will be arriving next week. Violet will likely—"

He looked to his daughter, stopping for a moment before continuing with his tale.

"Well, that is, Violet might stay on here."

"I see," Owen said slowly. "Well, it is unfortunate you will be selling the place. Your inn has been quite the respite to all who have called it home for the past few months. I know the Crown has appreciated your generosity."

"Hopefully it can continue," Elias said. "After all that happened here last month, I realize they may not be as interested in sending fellows our way, but the blame can hardly be placed on our shoulders."

"Father!" Iris exclaimed when Elias looked over at Westwood, as though he wanted to blame his newest son-in-law but wasn't entirely sure how to do so. "It was no one's fault."

"Well," Elias began, "They followed your husband here, Iris, and then Violet fell for that charlatan posing as an English soldier, and then Mr. Ridlington here didn't say anything about his suspicions — though nor did you, Iris, so—"

"Well, I think there is enough blame to go around for all," Owen said with what he hoped was an easy smile. While it was certainly not his place to interfere, he couldn't help but speak when he felt Violet go rigid beside him at her father's words.

It was true, she certainly had fallen for the wrong man, but now wasn't the time to remind her of such — not when they were all sitting here. Did her father not know his daughter well enough to realize just how much his words were hurting her? Owen hardly knew her at all, and yet he could tell how much she would be bothered by it.

When he looked over at the young woman beside him, he couldn't help the protectiveness he felt for her — even if it was against her own father. It was a strange sensation. He had certainly played the role of protector before, but not typically for a woman he hardly knew, and definitely not in any sense beyond protection from any physical harm. He was getting far too involved here. In fact, he shouldn't be at this luncheon at all.

"Our apologies, Mr. Ridlington," Daisy said with a forced smile, misreading his discomfort. "I am sure my father didn't mean for it to sound as though he was blaming anyone."

"Actually, I—oof!"

No one had said anything to further counter their

ELLIE ST. CLAIR

father's words, but a thud came from under the table, and by the look that crossed Iris' face moments before she took a sip of the lemonade in front of her, he had a feeling that she had put an end to whatever was next going to come out of their father's mouth.

"Well, then," Daisy said as she folded her hands on the table in front of her. "How is everyone enjoying their meal?"

The remainder of the luncheon stayed fairly civil, and Owen wasn't sure whether to be relieved or disappointed. While he certainly didn't want any of the women to feel uncomfortable, this was the most entertainment he had encountered in months.

When they finally finished, however, something was nagging at him that he couldn't quite describe. He had a feeling, however, that it was something that was somehow going to come back and haunt him.

4

———————

Violet had thought that she couldn't have been any further embarrassed in front of Owen Ridlington. She was wrong.

So far, he had witnessed her choose to bestow her affections upon the most untoward man possible, had listened to her ramble away about a fictional story in the gardens, and now had sat through a luncheon in which her father basically accused him of bringing discord to the inn when all he had done was protect the lot of them.

She should leave it be, allow one of her sisters to explain things to him. Yet the moment their lunch was finished, she found that she couldn't help herself from following him down the path to the beach.

"Mr. Ridlington?" she called, and when he didn't turn, she hurried her steps and tapped him on the sleeve before she lost her courage. When he turned quickly, she stopped abruptly with a little jump.

"Miss Violet, what can I do for you?" he asked, and Violet wondered at the bit of a sparkle in his eye, but she continued, her words rushing forward.

"It's just that... I wanted to apologize," she said, her words stilted. "For my father. And the luncheon. And well, basically all that has occurred since your arrival."

She squeezed her hands tightly together so that she wouldn't flail them around, as she often did when she was nervous. She had never stood so close to the man before, and she hadn't realized how much he would tower over her. As friendly as he was, there was also something somewhat mysterious about him, as though he had secrets hidden behind his handsome face and dark beard. His hazel eyes bore into her in a way that both excited and unnerved her. Why, she had no idea. She supposed it was because she had been around very few men like him before.

"There is nothing for which to apologize," he said, and she nodded, noting that his words sounded quite patrician, and she wondered where he came from. "Is your father truly selling the inn?"

"I'm not sure if *selling* is the correct word," she said, unable to meet his eyes any longer as she looked down to the ground. "He will still be involved, but it will be managed by another. The son of one of his closest friends."

"In what capacity are you meaning to stay on?" he asked, and Violet had no idea what to say. That she might be the man's wife? She hadn't yet agreed to such a thing, however, so she was certainly not going to share such information with a man she hardly knew.

"That has not yet been entirely decided," she said truthfully. "As you must realize, I have nowhere else to go."

"I suppose one day you will be married," he said, and her stomach seemed to churn as her ears grew hot. Why, she had no idea, for she had spoken of this many times before with her sisters and never had the subject caused such a reaction within her. It must be because now she might actually follow through with such a thing if she were to marry Linus.

"Perhaps," she said before wiping her now-perspiring hands on her skirts. "Well, then, I shall be off. Good day to you, Mr. Ridlington."

Violet began to walk away, but a strong, firm hand suddenly grasped her arm and she turned back to Mr. Ridlington in surprise.

"My apologies," he said, "But one more thing before you go."

"Yes?"

"The... unfortunate situation with Mr. Cooper— that is, the one in which he attempted to woo you—"

Violet swallowed hard. Why on earth was he speaking to her of this?

"I believe you were brave, to go with your sister to rescue Lord Westwood. Not many women would do such a thing."

"Not many women would have been so deceived by a man like Mr. Cooper — or, Comtois, I suppose I should call him — either," she said, hearing the bitterness on her tongue, but unable to do anything about it. The spy had lied to her and she had fallen for it, simply because she had been shocked that a good-looking man could actually be interested in her.

"He was a skilled liar. He came here with this intention," Mr. Ridlington said, and Violet attempted what she hoped was a polite smile.

"I appreciate the thought, Mr. Ridlington," she said. "Thank you."

She turned and forced herself to keep a reasonable pace as she returned to the inn. Why this man caused her to be so disconcerted, she had no idea. He was just another guest, another soldier. Although he was a handsome guest, that she couldn't deny. There was something about him that made her heart beat just a little faster. Which was ridiculous. She had hardly noticed him until recently, despite the fact he had been staying with them for some time now. Of course, she had thought she was attracted to another for a time, which seemed to have blinded her to all others.

But clearly, her own judgment was questionable, and she had vowed that she would never again be drawn in by an attractive man just because he showed her the slightest bit of interest.

No, she told herself, steeling her resolve. Owen Ridlington was handsome all right, but he was just a guest. Nothing more. If she was to marry, it would be to Linus.

So why did that thought fill her with dread?

~

THERE WAS one saving grace of being attached to this town for so long, Owen mused as he looked down at his scuffed boots the next day while he made his way to the stables next door.

It was that he had ample time to spend with his horse, Merlin. He had ridden the chestnut into town, and he was glad now he had chosen to bring his favorite mount along. He hadn't realized at the time how long he would be here, but a couple of months later this was beginning to feel much more permanent.

He was coming up behind the stable when he heard female voices beyond it.

"Just mount it, Vi." That was Iris.

"You have to learn at some point in time. Why not now? What if you ever need to ride alone?" Daisy.

"I have not had any need to until this point in time. I hardly see why I need to start now." And Violet.

"What if you have to go somewhere alone?" Iris asked. "You can hardly walk everywhere."

"That has served me just fine throughout my life," Violet replied.

"Yes, because we have always been here with you," Iris said. "You will be alone soon, once we leave, and you will more than likely have a need to ride alone. Come. Up you go."

He should leave them be. This had nothing to do with him, and he should walk by the meadow and continue on to his own horse. But he just couldn't help himself. Owen turned the corner and braced his shoulder against the fence in order to better watch the entertainment in front of him.

Violet stood before her mount, arms crossed in front of her as she eyed it. A sidesaddle sat on top of the sturdy brown horse with black stockings, who stared lazily back at her, clearly not regarding the situation with the same seriousness as Violet.

Her hair was back away from her face but a bonnet covered it, which didn't allow Owen to see the full range of her expressions. She wore a skirt of some kind of serviceable material along with her blouse, and he grinned as she began to speak.

"Sally," she said, holding up a finger, "you know that I am not entirely thrilled about this situation. When I climb up, *do not move*. Do you understand?"

"Vi," Marigold said, taking a step forward, "Perhaps it might be better if you are not quite so... abrupt with the horse."

"Oh, for goodness sake, Marigold, Sally doesn't understand what Violet is saying," Iris said in exasperation.

"I believe she does. At the very least, Violet's tone—"

"Violet, just mount the horse already," Daisy interjected, and Violet dropped her arms and sighed as she approached her.

"Very well."

Violet stepped forward and grasped the pommel before lifting her foot into the stirrup at Sally's side. She hoisted herself into the saddle, and with some grace she was soon on the horse's back, though even from where he stood, Owen could see how white her fingers were where she continued to grip the pommel atop the saddle. He gave her credit for attempting what was clearly a fear of hers.

"Let go and hold onto the reins, Vi," Iris said.

"No."

"Violet, you must—"

"I said *no!*" she exclaimed in what Owen realized was the most emotion he had ever heard from her. Perhaps it was time he intervened. He pushed off the fence he had been leaning against and stepped forward.

"Good day, ladies."

"Oh, Mr. Ridlington!" Marigold exclaimed as the three women on the ground turned in unison. "I didn't see you there."

Violet's back was to him now, and she seemed to have no inclination to turn in his direction — likely because she was too afraid to move — but Owen noted how rigid her back became as she sat even straighter.

"I see you are attempting a riding lesson."

"Attempt would be the word for it," Iris muttered, and Owen chuckled.

"As it happens," he said, looking at each of them in turn, "I have some practice in instructing new riders."

"Do you, now?" Daisy said, her eyes lighting up. "Well, then, you are likely far more qualified than we are."

"You told me that you knew what you were doing!" Violet said from the horse, and her sisters looked slightly chastised.

"We would have figured it out," Iris said with a grin, "But if Mr. Ridlington has a better suggestion…"

"Actually, why do I not take over from you?" he asked, and the sisters exchanged glances with one another.

"Well, we do have a few other things we should see to…" Iris said, biting her lip.

"The two of you run along," Daisy said. "I'll stay nearby in case Violet needs anything. Would that be all right, Mr. Ridlington?"

"Just fine," he said with a nod. "Not to worry, your sister is in good hands."

As the women walked away, though not without a few backward glances, he rounded the horse to stand in front of it so that Violet could see him.

"Now, Miss Violet," he said with a smile. "Let's start with a question."

"You really do not have to do this," she said with a slightly pained expression. "I'm sure you have many other things to do which would be far preferable to this."

"Not at all," he assured her. "I am more than happy to assist. Now tell me, why are you so frightened?"

"I am not frightened."

He said nothing but raised his eyebrows at her as he patted the horse's neck.

"Very well," she said with a sigh. "I fell off once when I was younger. I wasn't seriously injured, but it was enough of a scare that I don't like to ride alone."

"How did you fall?"

She looked directly into his eyes then, and he was startled by the intensity of her gaze.

"We were visiting with friends of my father's. As I was riding, one of the sons stepped out in front of the horse with a loud shout and spooked it. The horse bucked and I fell right off."

She bit her lip.

"I know it wasn't the horse's fault, and yet, I am aware that such a thing could happen again at any time."

"Well, Miss Violet," he said, "Children can do cruel things sometimes for no reason whatsoever. But let me tell you something. This horse you are on now looks to be a fairly safe bet. She seems unconcerned about the death grip you have upon her pommel, which is something to be said. Animals can sense your emotions. Until you can trust yourself, trust your horse. Here," he stepped closer to her and put his hands over hers, "let's try holding the reins, now shall we?"

She stared at him for a moment before finally offering a mute nod. She allowed him to lift her hands up and transfer them to the reins. Her skin underneath his was soft and warm, and he had to fight the instinct to wrap his hands around hers.

"You've ridden before, then. Do you recall the particulars?"

She nodded.

"All right then," he said. "Let's get you moving."

He walked the horse forward, and she followed obediently. It wasn't long — a few turns around the meadow — before he had her trotting along, and even though her eyes were still wide, her knuckles white with their grip, her jaw was now clenched in determination.

"I'm sending you alone now," he said, and when she

nodded, he let go. As he watched her sit up tall on the horse while they moved around the meadow, he was filled with pride at how well she was doing. It was slightly ridiculous to feel such a way, but he couldn't help himself.

And when she circled back, the smile that now glowed upon her face filled him with more joy than anything else had of late. Which scared him. His life was not one that allowed for any type of romance, which was beside the fact that he had no idea how she might respond to such an idea.

He had to be rid of these feelings, and fast. He could only see one way — by staying away from the woman.

So why was it proving so hard?

5

"How was the riding lesson?"

Violet halted suddenly in her steps and looked up, startled when Iris' voice invaded the story that was leaping off the pages in front of her. She had been so engrossed in the tale that she hadn't seen her sister standing in front of the bookshelf in the corner of the sitting room.

"My goodness, Iris, you startled me."

"Well, I can imagine so. You have your nose buried so deep in the pages within your hands that I cannot imagine how you see where you are going at all."

"As it happens, I do perfectly well at walking and reading at the same time. In fact, I can do nearly anything while I read the book."

"Except riding a horse and conversing with a handsome man."

"Handsome?"

"Yes. Your Mr. Ridlington."

Violet's cheeks warmed.

"He certainly is not *my* Mr. Ridlington, Iris. He is simply a guest at the inn."

"One who has taken considerable interest in you."

"He pities me, more than anything," Violet said, biting her lip, as she knew her words to be true. There was nothing between her and Mr. Ridlington, as Iris continued to suggest. No, the truth was far sadder. For she did feel something for him. He had awakened in her an attraction to a man unlike anything she had ever felt before. Certainly nothing like what she had thought she felt for Mr. Cooper, the man who had turned out to be a traitor and was simply using her for information about the inn and its guests. She knew now that she had simply been infatuated by him, that she had allowed herself to be charmed by his attention. It was ridiculous, and a mistake that she would not be repeating.

Which was why when it came to this man...

"See, I knew it!" Iris exclaimed. "That dreamy look has come over your face once more. Deny it or not, you do feel something for the man, Violet, and he must feel the same. For he's hardly said a word to the rest of us, but I've seen the two of you speaking with one another."

"You are being ridiculous."

"I am not."

Violet rolled her eyes at her sister, choosing to ignore her and her remarks.

"I am going to the bookstore. Would you like to come?"

"I would hardly call it a bookstore."

"Fine, then. I am going to the book section of the general store after I finish this. Would you like to come with me?"

Iris pondered the request for a moment.

"I truly would like to, believe it or not. However, I

promised August that we would go walking this morning, as we always do."

Now it was Iris' turn for the dreamy look to come into her eyes as she spoke of her husband. "Have fun, though, Vi!"

Violet nodded, happy to see her sister leave. She had only a chapter left of her book and was eager to finish it, alone and uninterrupted. She didn't think her sisters would ever understand that to interrupt her when a book was nearly finished was torture of the highest order.

She settled into the big brown monstrosity of a chair where her father liked to sit and finished the story in beautiful silence.

IRIS WAS correct in the fact that the book selection at the general store was rather meager. However, what she was not aware of was that Mr. Tenanbaum, the owner, was a kindred spirit. He understood Violet's love of the written word and he was happy to order for her whatever she requested. It often took weeks to arrive, but Violet appreciated the effort he went to in order to appease her. She would buy books, but he also let her borrow them from time to time. No one else quite understood her penchant for them.

So she was startled when she entered the store and rounded the last bit of merchandise to where the books awaited in the back corner. For there stood a man browsing the selection in front of him. He was tall, lean and lanky, standing with a nonchalance of which she had become rather familiar as of late. Mr. Ridlington.

She should turn around and walk out of the store, leave before he knew she was here. But she couldn't help herself

— there was something she had to know. Her curiosity got the better of her, and she tiptoed up behind him until she was standing over his shoulder.

And gasped when he turned around suddenly and smiled at her.

"Hello, Miss Violet."

"Mr. Ridlington! I— that is, I didn't know, I was just— How did you know I was here?"

She thought she had been perfectly silent, but apparently, he was far more perceptive than she had given him credit for.

"My purpose is to watch for danger and to know all that is around me, Miss Violet," he said, tipping up his hat enough that she could see his dancing hazel eyes below it. "You may be light of step, but I still hear you."

"Oh," was all she said, and he smiled wider.

"Let me guess. You'd like to know what I am reading?"

"I, ah... yes, I would."

He held up the book in his hands.

"Nothing particularly exciting, as it were. The exploits of William Baffin."

"Oh, on the contrary, Mr. Ridlington — that book is quite exciting."

He looked surprised. "You've read it?"

"I believe our Violet here has read every book that I bring into the store."

Violet turned when she heard Mr. Tenanbaum. He hadn't been at the counter when she entered.

"Good day, Mr. Tenanbaum," she said with a sincere smile, for she always loved visiting with him. "How are you?"

"Just fine," he said, his returning smile covering his wrinkled face. "In fact, I was about to send word to you."

"Oh?"

"You'll never guess what came in — *Pride and Prejudice*."

"Truly?" she asked, excitement growing within her. "I thought it had sold out. I didn't think it would be possible."

"I do my best to find anything you request," he said as he handed her the book. "When you're done, I'll read it myself, and after that, it's yours."

"Whatever the price, I am happy to pay."

"It's a gift."

"Oh, Mr. Tenanbaum, I couldn't—"

"You will," he said, holding up a hand to stem her protest. "If it wasn't for you, Violet, I'd have no one in this village to discuss all of these tomes with that no one has touched in years but you."

Violet looked down at the floor with a small smile.

"Well, thank you again."

"And it seems you have a fellow reader here."

Violet looked over to Mr. Ridlington, who was watching their exchange with interest.

"Oh?"

"Yes, Mr. Ridlington has been in here every few days trying something new."

"You are not happy with the selection at the inn, Mr. Ridlington?" Violet asked. At first, he looked worried, taken aback at her apparent dismay, but after a moment he finally realized she was joking and his face broke out into an easy grin.

"You're jesting."

"I am," she said. "Did you not think I was capable of such a thing?"

"Not at all," he said, though his face belied his words.

"Well, I am happy to have surprised you."

When he smiled at her, she could hardly believe how

much that grin changed his looks. He was a handsome man, there was no doubt, but he was also somewhat unassuming. Then he smiled that slow, easy grin through his beard, causing his eyes to sparkle and his entire countenance to change. He winked at her now, and she nearly jumped, so startled was she by how much his gesture sent a thrilling shock through her from the top of her spine down and out the tips of her toes.

"Violet," he said, stretching her name out, and she loved how it sounded coming off of his lips. "May I call you Violet?"

"Yes, of course, everyone does."

His eyes seemed to darken and he nodded. "Thank you. I—"

But before he could say another word, their attention was directed to the door, through which a man hurriedly entered. His attire was disheveled, his hat askew, but he seemed quite determined.

"Lord Primrose?" he called out. "Is there a Lord Primrose here?"

No one in the store said anything for a moment, and finally Violet stepped forward.

"I am very sorry, but I do not believe there is anyone in this town by such a name."

"I was told he is staying at the inn; however when I arrived there after much confusion I was told he could be found here. The matter is quite urgent, I can assure you. I—"

"I am Lord Primrose."

Violet blinked, startled. It sounded like Mr. Ridlington had spoken. But that couldn't be. For he was simply Mr. Ridlington, not—

"Here you are, my lord," the messenger said, passing

him the paper he held in front of him. "Best read it quickly. I'll remain here until you have time to craft a response."

"Very well," Mr. Ridlington— er, Lord Primrose— said with a nod before he turned to Violet and Mr. Tenanbaum. "My apologies. I must be going. My reading selection will have to wait for another time."

Then, before Violet could gather her wits, he was out of the store and walking back down the street toward the inn. She swallowed hard. Lord Primrose? He was a member of the nobility and he had never mentioned such, not even once, to any of them? What was he trying to hide?

Mr. Tenanbaum cleared his throat, and Violet realized that she was staring after Mr. Ridlington— or, she should say, Lord Primrose. She gathered her wits to herself and turned back to the counter.

"Thank you again, Mr. Tenanbaum, for bringing this in for me. I will be sure to return it for your own reading as soon as I can."

"Enjoy it, Violet," he said as she began walking toward the door. "Oh, and Violet? I'm sure your Lord Primrose there had a reason for not telling you who he was. Likely didn't want to seem too pretentious or some such thing."

"Of course," she said with a forced smile, but she wasn't so sure as she pushed open the door and followed his footsteps down the street.

6

The boarders and family gathered together in the guest sitting room reminded Violet of another time which had been equally horrific — when they had been together for the musicale at which she and her sisters had to provide the entertainment.

But that was a story for another day, and today they had much larger concerns if the look upon Lord Primrose's face was any indication.

He stood at the front of the room, leaning against the wall. Despite his stance, his eyes were alert as they moved over the lot of them gathered within the room. There were six other former soldiers, her sisters' husbands, and her own family.

"I have received a missive," he said, tipping his hat away from his face, "and the news is somewhat troubling."

Violet bit her lip. Whatever this news was, would he be leaving? Though that concern should be far from her thoughts. Why did it matter at all?

"Some of you may know of Comtois, who stayed here a

few months ago. He originally went by 'Mr. Cooper,' until his true identity as a French spy was discovered."

Violet looked down at her hands. Unfortunately, she knew more about Comtois than she would have liked.

"Well," he said, drawling the word out much to the dismay of all who were awaiting him to speak, "It seems that Comtois has escaped his containment."

"What?" came the outspoken cry around the room, Iris' being the loudest, which was understandable. The man had captured and attempted to kill the man who was now her husband, after all.

Lord Primrose cringed, clearly not relishing being the one to share the news.

"He apparently faked an illness. His guards thought he was dying. When they rushed in to help, he was ready and able to escape."

"While we do not wish to hear of a prisoner escaping, what does that mean for us?" asked one of the soldiers who was convalescing at the inn.

"The trouble is that Comtois knows all about The Wild Rose Inn," Lord Primrose said with an apologetic look at the family. "Not only that, but he now has his own vendetta and wishes to see the inn — and the Tavners family — come to harm. We have no idea where he is, and if or when he might return here."

"Good heavens!" Violet's mother exclaimed with a bit of a shriek and much trepidation in her voice. "That is *most* troubling. Whatever are we to do?"

"Now see here," Violet's father, Elias, said, standing. "That is certainly not what I signed up for. I was told that the inn would remain shrouded in secrecy, that we had nothing to worry about."

"I am sure those promises were made with the best of

intentions," Lord Primrose said calmly. "However, sometimes, especially in war, circumstances change."

"Well, I will not stand for this!" raged Elias, but Lord Primrose continued speaking in his matter-of-fact tone.

"Unfortunately, there is nothing we can do now — but defend this inn," he said, setting his jaw stoically. "I have a plan. There are not many of us here, but the ten of us, and anyone else from the village who will volunteer must create a militia. We will defend this inn from any who attempt to do it harm, until such time that the threat no longer exists. In fact, I suggest that we get the word out and begin training this very afternoon."

"Perhaps we should all just leave," Alice exclaimed. "My daughters each have substantial homes."

"You are more than welcome to do so, Alice," Violet's father's voice boomed. "But I will stay here and defend what is mine!"

Violet exchanged a worried glance with her sisters, embarrassed at their parents' argument in front of the other men who were gathered here. On one point her mother, however, was right.

The sisters gathered together off to the side for a private discussion. Violet turned to Marigold, who was sitting next to her. "You should go, "she said, "Especially you, in your expectant condition."

"I agree," Marigold said with a nod. "And you all will come with us."

"I cannot," Violet said with a shake of her head. "Someone needs to see to the inn and the guests. We know that Father could never do it, and it would be best Mother leave as well."

"You will not stay here alone!"

"Father will be here."

"Yes, but—"

"August and I will stay," Iris said resolutely. "I'm sure he will feel responsible."

"Nonsense," Violet said.

It was then that they noticed the makeshift meeting had begun to break up, and the men were beginning to consult one another about their next plans. Daisy's husband, the Duke of Greenwich, and Lord Westwood were actively in the conversation, though Marigold's husband, Lord Dorchester, looked worriedly back at his wife.

"Go," Daisy urged. "We shall be fine."

Marigold placed her hands over her stomach before looking up, though her worried expression remained.

"Very well," she said, biting her lip. "But I don't like this."

And though she agreed with her sister, somehow, with Lord Primrose here, Violet didn't feel worried at all.

∼

DESPITE HIS BEST EFFORTS, Owen could not convince the family to leave.

"How are the soldiers supposed to function if they do not have clean linens and food upon the table?" Daisy argued as only the family remained in the room with him.

"I will have the maids do it," Elias Tavners said, but Violet shook her head.

"We cannot ask them to stay when we ourselves would go. That would be cowardly."

Owen was impressed with her compassion, but slightly frustrated with it as well.

"Marigold and her husband are packing at this moment," Daisy said. "Which is wise, with the babe and

Dorchester's inability to fight due to his injuries, anyway. The rest of us will stay here and watch out over this place."

Owen realized he wasn't getting anywhere with his argument, and finally relented.

"Fine," he said. "But please, will you promise to stay out of the way of the men's training? I wouldn't like anyone to be injured. And one more thing."

They all looked at him expectantly.

"It would be best if you all learned to defend yourself as well."

"Oh, exciting!" Iris said, and he looked over at her.

"I realize this may seem somewhat of a thrill, but this must be taken seriously. For all we know, Comtois may return to France and forget he ever knew anything about The Wild Rose Inn. But we must be prepared should that not be the case."

The women's faces turned serious — though Violet's had been from the beginning. Although she was rather quiet and seemed to defer to her sisters, there was an inner strength about her that was slowly revealing itself to him, a side that Owen wanted to know much more about.

As the family began to return to their own quarters, Owen stepped forward and placed a hand on Violet's arm.

"Would you have a moment for a quick word?" he murmured, and she nodded. He saw her sisters look back at her with some question, but she motioned for them to continue on without her.

Seeing that some of the other soldiers remained, Owen led her out the back door of the inn to the gardens. The sun was just beginning to set from behind the inn, and Violet's face was bathed in a beautiful golden glow that shone off of her cheekbones, her unexpected beauty becoming so enchanting that Owen nearly lost his train of thought.

"Miss Violet—"

"Violet."

"Violet, yes," he said, clearing his throat. He was making a mess of this. And why? It was not as though he ever had a particularly difficult time speaking to a young woman.

"I realize that you were rather... surprised to hear me addressed as Lord Primrose."

She nodded, but looked down at a point somewhere on his chest, not meeting his eyes. "I was, my lord, and am rather embarrassed that I — and my family — have referred to you as Mr. Ridlington since you arrived."

He waved a hand in the air. "Nothing to be embarrassed about. How could you be, when I was the one who neglected to mention such a thing?"

"Is there a reason you hid your title from us?" she asked, meeting his eye now.

"Not at all," he said with a shrug. "I was introduced as Owen Ridlington and left it at that. My title has nothing to do with the role I am to serve here, and I would rather not mention it when it's not warranted. I would prefer to know more about the goings on around Southwold, and it is easier when one is not seen as a peer."

"I suppose I can understand that," she said slowly. "What am I to tell my family?"

Owen was relieved that, from her question, she had apparently not mentioned anything yet.

"I would prefer to remain Owen Ridlington, if you feel comfortable in not saying anything further."

"I would not lie if I was asked, but I do not see any issue in not mentioning what I know."

"Thank you, Violet."

Her cheeks turned quite a pretty pink suddenly as she looked at him with some intent.

"And how am I to refer to you now?"

"I think Owen will suffice. It will make things slightly less confusing."

The corners of her lips turned up into a small smile that was just for him, as though they shared a secret of which no one else was a part.

"Very well... Owen."

He had never thought much of his name — good nor bad, it was just his name. But now, hearing it upon her lips, he suddenly felt quite blessed that his parents had decided to name him such.

He cleared his throat.

"You'd best get your rest, for tomorrow we will begin practicing."

"Practicing?" she asked with a spark in her eyes, and suddenly he thought of all the things they could spend time becoming proficient at.

"On how to best defend yourself."

"Oh, yes, that's right," she said, her flaming cheeks causing a quickening of his heartbeat as he realized that she was thinking along the same lines as he. "I look forward to it."

He would have as well, were this under better circumstances. As it was, he was becoming concerned about the potential threat of Comtois and the French. Were it another stronghold he was defending, so be it, but to know that Violet — and her family — could be in danger was making him fearful. He did wish they had all taken his advice and relocated for a time, but he couldn't force them to move anywhere. He could only keep them safe.

And as his eyes followed after Violet re-entering the inn, he vowed to do just that.

7

_____

Owen looked around him at the meadow that was now filled with people. There were some of the villagers who had volunteered to be part of his militia, as it were, and then the Tavners family, who he would be training, though Elias Tavners seemed fairly sure of his own skill and ability to prepare the rest of his family.

As Owen watched him, however, he had his doubts.

"And this, Iris, is a pistol," Tavners said, though he then fumbled with the weapon as he attempted to determine just how it would fire. Owen sighed. Iris and Daisy's husbands were with the rest of the men, attempting to train them on the protocol if the enemy was spotted. The men had been out all morning, though the family had just arrived.

The problem was, they were unsure if Comtois would have returned to French soil to gather troops by boat, or if he had stayed in England and would be approaching over land. Tavners had told Owen that he would tour him around the outskirts of the town following the training session to determine the best lookout points. Owen had scouted the area quite often himself, but perhaps Tavners would have additional sites he had missed.

Owen returned to his newly formed army.

"Thank you, everyone, for your attention today. Southwold is in good hands with the likes of you, and soon enough we will be prepared for whatever comes our way. We will reconvene tomorrow to continue."

He turned toward the Tavners family now and took a deep breath. He was about to walk over to them when he felt a hand on his shoulder. He turned to find Daisy's husband, the Duke of Greenwich, beside him, looking at the family beyond.

"I think we should take this one-on-one," he said. "Best to allow Elias to think he's in charge. Westwood and I will help with our wives, leave Tavners to his own, and you can train Violet."

Suddenly Owen was not quite as hesitant about the task before him.

"Very well," he agreed. "Lead on."

Greenwich explained the plan to Tavners, who concurred. Owen walked over to Violet, who was looking at the knife and pistol in front of her with some trepidation.

"I'm assuming you have never fired a pistol before," he said with a bit of a smile, but she didn't see it as she was preoccupied with the instruments before her.

"I have not," she confirmed.

"Very well," he said. "Let us remedy that, shall we?"

He picked up the holster pistol, showed her how to load it, aim it, and pull the trigger. He aimed at the straw pallet targets he had set up earlier.

"Then it is simply a matter of pulling the trigger. It will be a moment until it actually fires."

She nodded.

"The only thing is..." she began.

"Yes?"

"What if I do not *want* to shoot anything? Do not misunderstand me, I understand how important it is to defend ourselves if it came to that, but I cannot imagine what it must be like to... to *kill* someone." Her eyes widened as though she was just reaching an understanding. "Have you?"

He could have pretended not to understand her meaning, but he chose instead to answer her.

"I have," he said with a nod.

"Do you not feel..." She trailed off, as though unable to even speak of what it must be like.

"Remorse? Of course I do. But if it is a matter of my own life or the life of a friend and that of an enemy... well, it makes the decision easier. Though still not a simple choice."

She nodded, contemplation upon her face.

"I understand that. I still, however, do not think I could do such a thing."

"Well, just in case," he said, putting the gun into her hand, "It's best you try."

They heard a shout of glee and looked over to see that Iris had connected with the target. That put a bit of fire in Violet's eye as she stepped up to shoot at the target beside her sister's.

She followed Owen's instructions, took aim, and pulled the trigger, widely missing the target in front of her.

"That's all right," he said. "Try again."

She lined up once more, and he saw that this shot would likely follow the last. He stood behind her, crouching down slightly so he had the same vantage point, and then placed one arm on hers, gently pushing it down so that she had better aim.

"See?" he said, and she nodded. When she did, the scent of cherry blossoms floated up into his nostrils, and he closed his eyes for a moment as he inhaled her sweet scent. Unlike the horrors of war he had seen so often as of late, this woman was a reminder of all that was good in the world. For a moment, Owen pictured her within his own home, standing at the door looking out to greet him, exuberant when he returned to her from wherever he had recently been posted.

But then he heard the bang of a nearby pistol, and he was reminded of what his world currently was. It was war, death, fighting. She should be as far removed from it as possible.

He wished she was now.

"Can I fire?" she asked softly, and he was brought back to the present.

"Yes," he said, stepping back from her. "Yes, of course."

She did so, her bullet hitting the very bottom of the target — but hitting it nonetheless.

"I did it!" she exclaimed, much more subdued than her sister but still, with excitement. Owen grinned.

"That you did," he said. "Impressive marksmanship."

She turned to him, her face sparkling with glee, but then their eyes met and suddenly her smile somewhat dimmed. But it wasn't as though she was upset. No... she bit her lip and her eyes darkened, and when she looked up at him, gone was the sweet, innocent woman and in her place was someone much more... seductive. Owen swallowed hard. He leaned in toward her, his only focus those soft pink lips, which he longed to taste.

And then there was another report from a gun, and they both jumped backward, remembering where they were, and that they were not alone.

She turned around suddenly, facing the target again, and it now felt as though he had no place for his hands, no idea what to do with himself.

"Best continue on," he finally said, and she nodded, leaving Owen to determine that perhaps it was time to find Elias.

"Tavners," he greeted the man, who looked positively exhausted as he attempted to show his wife the workings of the pistol in her hand. The way she was waving it around caused Owen to take a step backward so that if the thing were to go off he would be out of the line of fire. "Are you ready for our tour?"

"Tour?"

"We were going to go scout locations," Owen reminded him, and the man slapped a hand against his forehead.

"Ah, that's right!" he exclaimed. "The thing is, with all of this movement, my back has begun to ache something fierce."

He placed a hand on it as though it had just flared up.

"Another time?" Tavners asked, and Owen shrugged.

"Sure."

He would just have to go searching for himself.

"Perhaps I can help?'

They both turned to see Violet standing there, looking hesitant and unsure of herself, but Owen seized upon her offer. He would prefer to have Violet as a guide over her father any day.

"Wonderful," he said before Tavners could say anything. He offered his arm. "Shall we go?"

~

WHAT HAD SHE JUST DONE?

Violet had overheard Owen speaking with her father, and suddenly the prospect of spending an afternoon alone with him was more enticing than she could bear. The words had flown out, and now... now she was regretting she had ever opened her mouth. For after that moment between her and Owen a few minutes ago, what would happen when they were truly alone?

The thought filled her with trembling.

Oh, how she sometimes wished she could be like Iris, eagerly taking advantage of such situations when they came her way. Iris would know what to say, how to handle herself.

Perhaps, Violet thought, she could attempt to take on the personality of a character from one of her books. She would be witty and laugh when it was appropriate, flirt outrageously, and convince the man to fall in love with her.

But was that what she wanted? She had thought she had desired such a thing with the man who had turned out to be a French spy. Was Owen any better? For he was not going to be staying here at the inn forever, and his only interest in her seemed to be in protecting her.

It was, however, too late to back out of her promise now. Violet swallowed her fear and placed what she hoped was a convincing smile on her face as she looked up at him.

"Yes," she said as decisively as she could. "We shall."

8

_____

"If nothing else, today will be a good test of your newly acquired skills on horseback," Owen said, and Violet stopped, turning to him.

"On horseback?" she asked, immediately realizing that she sounded ridiculous. Of course, they would go on horseback. They could hardly tour around the town and its vantage points on foot.

"Yes," he said, and if Violet wasn't mistaken, she thought one corner of his mouth was beginning to curl beneath his beard. "Is that not where we were headed — to the stable?"

"Of course," she said, attempting to cover her surprise.

"It will be a good opportunity for me to allow Merlin to stretch his legs," Owen continued, and Violet simply nodded. For it was as she suspected. When she exited the stable and clumsily mounted Sally, she looked over at Owen on his magnificent horse. She must look utterly ridiculous next to him. They hardly made a fitting pair. Owen didn't seem to think anything of it, however, as he reined in his horse next to her.

"Well," he said, "where to first?"

Violet shook the cobwebs from her mind as she determined a plan for them for the next hour or so and then recited it to Owen, who seemed to agree with her. She wondered that he hadn't already scouted the area — was that not his purpose here? But if he wanted a local's point of view, then she was happy to contribute. She first led him to the various high points on the cliffs where one could see out over the water.

They sat atop their horses, staring out over the bay. The gentle breeze brushed against Violet's cheek, and she pushed her bonnet back to hang behind her neck as she closed her eyes to feel the sun upon her face and the wind in her hair.

"I do hope Southwold does not become a place of battle," she said softly, hardly realizing at first that she had spoken the thought aloud. "It is such a peaceful town, I would hate for violence to fall upon it again."

"Again?" Owen questioned, and Violet nodded.

"Over one hundred years ago — in May of 1672 — there was a major battle upon these waters below us."

"Ah, yes, I believe I read of such. Against the Dutch, was it not?"

"It was," she said, smiling at him, pleased he knew of some of the town's history. "The English and French were actually fighting together at that point in time. The English fleet was in Southwold on a sort of leave — most of their time was spent within the alehouses. A French frigate arrived in the wee hours of the night to warn that the Dutch Fleet had been sighted and would be upon them shortly. In a few hours, the English ships were at sea, commanded by the Duke of York and the Earl of Sandwich. The French, as it were, sailed away, leaving the English to fend for themselves." She paused in her tale to smile wryly at that.

"There were seventy-one English ships to the Dutch's sixty-one. The battle was fairly even and raged through the day. People gathered on these very cliffs to watch the battle, but little could be seen for the ships were ten miles from land. Villagers were told to remain, in case the Dutch made it ashore and they would have to fight. Thankfully, it never came to pass — as hopefully will happen at this particular time as well."

"Who won the battle?"

"The English say they did. Though each side lost two ships and about 2000 men. It is said bodies washed ashore for days — including the Earl of Sandwich's."

She winced at the thought. "The people of Southwold had to care for over 800 injured sailors."

"You know much of this town's history," Owen acknowledged, and Violet was suddenly embarrassed by how she had droned on about the battle.

"I suppose I do," she said with a shrug. "I love this town and I love reading about history, so I suppose it has stayed in my mind. Anyway, if you are going to see anything, it would be from here. You do not think the French would actually sail upon us here, do you? Just for our little inn and a few men?"

"I doubt it," he said. "I do not think the French will bother much with us if I am being honest. Lord Westwood may hold some information, but he likely would have shared it by now if that was the case. No, my guess is that, if anything, Comtois himself may arrive here for personal vengeance. Perhaps we best concentrate farther inland now."

"Very well," she said, turning the horse and leading him toward the wooded area near the Southwold road.

"You're riding well," he said, and Violet laughed softly.

"We are simply walking," she said. "That does not require much skill."

"You should be proud of your abilities," Owen said, "For it means I did my job as a teacher."

"Oh, I wouldn't question any of your skills or accomplishments," Violet said shyly, and Owen chuckled.

"You do not know me well, then."

"I suppose I don't," Violet said, and they lapsed into silence for a moment, as all she could think about was the fact that she would like to.

She slowed Sally as they approached the main road.

"This, of course, is where most enter Southwold if coming by land," she said. "However, there is another path — one that is not often used, and which a carriage could never fit through. A man on horseback, however, likely could."

Owen's eyes lit up. "I didn't know about this."

She nodded. "Most wouldn't, unless one is from here."

"Ernest Abernathy is."

Violet nodded. Ernest was the son of the apothecary and had become involved in the nefarious plans of Comtois for revenge against Lord Westwood.

"He could have told Comtois of the path, though hopefully he never thought to do so. We can ride the horses around to find it, or we can walk and lead them through the woods to get there more quickly."

"Very well," Owen said. "Show me the way."

They dismounted, and Violet did her best to remember the most direct route to the path. It had been some years since she had taken this way, which they sometimes used as a shortcut to get in and out of town.

She pushed tree branches aside as she walked, holding them back to allow Sally through as well as Owen leading Merlin behind her. She heard him mutter as she accidentally let one go and it slapped him in the face.

"I'm sorry," she said.

"Think nothing of it," he said with a shake of his head as they continued on.

"Here it is!" she exclaimed when she saw the packed ground in front of her. It wasn't much but tamped-down grass that twisted around the trees in the wood, but it would lead someone into town if nothing else.

Violet turned to continue down the path until they reached the entrance where it emerged to join with the main road itself.

"This is where it begins," she said, and Owen nodded.

"Perfect," he said, his smile of pleasure warming her through. "I shall station one of the men here to keep watch."

"Thank you," she said, turning to him, startled to find that he was just behind her. She took the slightest step back but bumped into Sally.

"I deserve no thanks," he said, his brow furrowing. "We brought this upon you. Southwold would not be threatened if it wasn't for the fact that you were housing former soldiers."

"Which my father more than welcomed," she reminded him.

"That, I do not completely understand," Owen said with a frown. "Considering he had four daughters at home."

"He loved the idea of having the opportunity to converse with soldiers once more," Violet said. "And then there is his compensation from the army. My father...

enjoys the odd game of chance that typically does not end well for him."

"I see," Owen said, and Violet could tell that he now understood her father's motives far better. "I am sorry to hear it."

"We are getting by now, at least," she said, attempting nonchalance. "And we strongly discourage him from gambling. My new brothers-in-law have done better at keeping him in line. Which is something else — had we not housed the soldiers, my sisters would never have found their husbands."

"They do all seem happy," Owen noted. "That is a rare occurrence, I have found."

"This is true," Violet said with a smile, as she truly was pleased for her sisters.

"You deserve happiness, yourself, Violet," Owen said, tilting his head ever so slightly as he contemplated her. "Will you be happy, remaining here with the new owner of the inn?"

If only he knew of her father's plans.

"I don't know," she said honestly. "I try not to hold too high a hope for whatever the future might hold for me, be it at the inn or... somewhere else."

"Where else would you like to go?" he asked, scrutinizing her more closely. Violet longed to say that she had a penchant to be with him, to see where he might take her, but how could she do so when he might laugh at such an idea, or, even worse, look upon her solely with pity?

She bit her lip. "I suppose I would like to go see some of the places that I have visited through the pages of my books."

"Is that all?"

"What do you mean?"

"Books offer more than travel. They contain relationships, myriad emotions, adventure, and... love."

Violet swallowed hard at the intense look within his eyes, unsure of what to read into his words.

"They do," she said, her voice just over a whisper, and Owen reached out slowly, lifting a hand to her face and stroking her cheek with his roughened fingers, sending chills through her body.

When she leaned her face into his touch, he raised his other hand so that he was cupping her cheeks, and then, so slowly it seemed nearly a dream, he leaned toward her, tilting her face up to his, until their lips softly brushed against one another — once, twice, and then as one they pressed into one another, the kiss deepened to one that was far more than affection.

Violet's heart nearly exploded with joy and exhilaration as her body longed to do the same. She lifted her arms to wrap them around Owen's neck, and he responded by removing a hand from her face to encircle it around her waist and pull her up against him. His lips slanted over hers again and again, until she opened her mouth and he plundered that as well.

Violet had never been kissed and had certainly never imagined it would be possible to be kissed like this. Owen seemed to know exactly what to do to allow her to feel incredibly and impossibly cherished.

What seemed like mere moments later, yet in the same breath could have been hours, they broke away from one another. Violet was embarrassed by how fast her breath stole in and out, until she realized that Owen's was the same. She looked up, meeting his eyes as incredulity stole over her. For he seemed as affected as she was, his gaze befuddled. Was this always how a kiss affected one? Or was it

Owen... or the two of them together? She hardly had words to explain her turmoil. She only knew she longed for it once more.

"That was..." she began then shook her head, mute, unable to finish the sentence.

"Perfect," he finished, with a smile, and then took her hand, bringing it to his lips for a kiss. Violet didn't think she would ever be the same again.

9

Owen knew he should be solely concentrating on his efforts of protecting Southwold and its people, particularly the inhabitants of the inn. Never had he had more purpose for which to offer his protection than now.

Except that he could hardly think of anything but Violet Tavners.

She was unlike any woman he had ever met before. She was quiet and unassuming, yet she held within her such a vast amount of knowledge, intelligence, and, it seemed, passion.

He drew a deep breath. Women didn't typically affect him so much. In fact, there wasn't much of anything that usually ruffled him. He was the one others came to when they wanted sound judgment and sensible advice. He certainly was not the type to allow his heart to rule his head.

He enjoyed women as much as any man, had made the casual acquaintance in the past, but never had Owen allowed himself to get close. For his work in this war was not conducive to having a wife at home waiting for him. He was barely ever there, for one thing, and for another, there was the simple fact that one day he might not return from a mission.

Owen tipped his hat back on his head as he approached the inn. The day following his excursion with Violet, he had spent the morning with his newly formed militia once more, though his mind was elsewhere — it was back at the entrance to that path in the woods, with her.

They had returned to the inn following that kiss, making easy conversation, with small, secret smiles sent back and forth. Owen had expected Violet to shy away from him following their kiss, but instead, she seemed rather enamored with the whole situation, which only called to him all the more.

He wiped his forehead. It had been a long day. Most of the soldiers within the inn were already battle -weary and did not require much training, but their motivation was certainly lacking. They had assumed their fighting days were behind them.

The local men... well, they were eager all right, but most of them hardly knew which side of the gun to point straight ahead.

He pushed open the door to the inn, ready to sit down for a good meal and rest for a few hours before he would begin to keep watch for the night. His eyes were nearly closing following his lack of sleep over the previous two nights, and he almost walked into the back of a man standing in the middle of the foyer.

"Excuse me," he murmured, and the man turned to face him.

"Careful now," he said, and Owen raised his eyebrows. This must be someone new to the inn, but he didn't look like any soldier Owen had ever seen. His clothing was crisp, clean, and of the latest fashions, though not of the most expensive cloths. His eyes ran up and down Owen's well-worn pants and linen shirt, and Owen wanted to laugh at the fact that this man clearly thought himself to be his superior.

"You must be new here," Owen said, taking the higher road and holding out his hand. "Owen Ridlington."

The man eyed his calloused hand with distaste but finally took it, his hands soft and the shake limp.

"Mr. Linus Anderson."

"What brings you to The Wild Rose Inn?" Owen asked, wary of the newcomer, as he typically would be no matter the circumstance, but particularly today.

The man seemed to attempt to stand taller.

"I will be running this inn fairly soon."

"Ah," Owen said, remembering Elias Tavners' announcement. His first thought was for Violet and what it would be like for her to work with such a man. "Then congratulations are in order."

"You are aware of my forthcoming marriage, then?"

"Your marriage?" Owen asked, confused. "My apologies, but no. I was congratulating you as successor of the inn."

"Right, right," Anderson said. "Well, with the inn comes a beautiful maiden. I am told I shall have the youngest as the other three have already been married off. They are all beauties, however, so that should not be an issue. In fact, I am looking forward to inspecting the woman."

A hard ball of jealous anger began to form in Owen's stomach. Marriage to the youngest? Why was he speaking of her as though she were livestock? He certainly better not be talking about—

But then he heard a noise from the room's entrance, and he turned to find Violet standing within the doorway. Her violet eyes were wide in her ashen face as she took in the pair of them standing there. She had clearly heard Anderson's words, but her gaze was upon Owen instead of the other man.

"Violet," he said, ignoring Anderson. "Is what he says true?"

He saw her throat move as she swallowed, but she answered him.

"Not exactly," she said, her eyes now flicking over to Anderson. "It is... potentially an option."

Linus laughed. "Is that what you've been told? No, my dear. I am in need of a wife, and I was promised you. If your father would like someone to take over this inn, then I shall require your services as well."

"My services?" Violet squeaked.

"Why, yes. I certainly can't run this place myself. Were you not told the terms of the agreement?"

Violet looked as though she was about to keel over. Owen was torn between the urge to move to her and hold her up or to run from the room and this town and never look back. He shouldn't be dallying with her as it was, but now with the knowledge that she could be promised to another...

Elias Tavners chose that moment to finally walk into the foyer, and Violet stepped aside, allowing her father to greet Anderson as though he was his own long-lost child. Violet stepped back and over to Owen, looking up at him with desperate eyes.

"Can we have a moment alone? Outside perhaps?"

Owen bristled but gave a quick, firm nod, placing a hand at the small of her back, unable to prevent the twinge of affection when he felt her softness beneath the rough wool of her work dress.

They stepped outside, the brilliant colors of the garden, the smell of the ocean spray, and the call of the birds bringing a temporary peace. Owen closed his eyes to allow the ire that Anderson's presence brought forth to slowly seep away.

"Owen," Violet said, causing his eyes to open. Her plaintive look, her wide, pleading eyes in her round, pretty face called him to listen to her words. "What Linus said inside... that was not my understanding of the situation."

"Linus?" he questioned, raising an eyebrow at the use of his given name.

"We knew one another as children, so that is what I remember him as," she explained with a heavy sigh. "I have not seen him in years. Before... a week ago, my father told me that he would like to see the inn pass on to Linus, and to solidify the arrangement, I was to marry him. I wasn't sure if I would ever find a man who I could hold true affection for, or who would see me in equal light. I told my father that I would decide whether or not I would agree to such a thing *after* Linus arrived, once I had the opportunity to come to know him better. Apparently... that was not what Linus has agreed to."

She paused for a moment. "Or perhaps my father was simply placating me by telling me it was my decision to make when that was not the case at all."

Her eyes filled with tears, and Owen couldn't help but allow his heart to go out to her, though his opinion of her father was lowering even further by the moment.

"Why did you not tell me of him and this... arrangement?" he asked, attempting to keep emotion out of this conversation.

"At first... well, I had no reason to. To be honest, I was somewhat embarrassed by the fact that this was apparently my only option for marriage. My sisters were able to marry for love, whereas I... well, my affections were so misplaced in the past that I doubted whether I would ever have the same opportunity."

She shifted her gaze downward, as though unable to meet his eyes, and all he could see were the gold streaks shining through her soft brown hair as he found himself without words.

"Then you and I became close so suddenly. With everything else that was happening around us, I suppose I didn't know how to bring it up, or even if I should."

Owen nodded, the sincerity of her words stirring him. "I understand."

"You do?" She looked back up at him, her luminous eyes shimmering with tears.

"Of course," he said with a shrug. "I am not an unreasonable man. Though the situation is rather.... unfortunate."

She made a noise that was half-laugh, half-sob, and then brought her hand to her mouth as though to cover it. "You could say so."

"What will you do?" he asked, pulling the brim of his hat lower over his face.

"I have no idea."

It was certainly not the answer he was hoping to hear. Though if he were being honest with himself, what would he have her say? That she wanted to decline this Anderson fellow and be with him instead? He had nothing to offer her at this point in time except perhaps a promise for the possible future. And he could not ask her to wait for a day that might never come.

But nor did he have it within him, at least at this very moment, to tell her to marry the man. Owen had not had much of a conversation with him, but from what he had witnessed, he wasn't impressed.

He stretched his hand out, palm facing up, toward Violet. She looked down at it for a moment before reaching out and placing her soft, small hand within his. He wrapped his fingers around it, for a moment simply marveling at the difference between the two of them. He looked back up at her with what he hoped was an encouraging smile.

"There is much to be resolved," he said softly. "We will first worry about your safety and that of all at the inn, and by then you should know what to do about your Mr. Anderson. Tell me, do you love this place?"

"It is home," was all she said. "It is all I know."

She had not answered his question, but he let it go and instead simply squeezed her hand. "Whether or not you remain here, let's keep this place safe for now. I wonder if Mr. Anderson is aware—"

"Just what do you mean by *dangerous situation*?" The angry bellow came from inside of the inn, and Owen chuckled.

"It seems he knows of the threat now. Come, we best go see whether or not he will be staying, and if the man knows how to defend himself."

Violet nodded, steeled her shoulders, and led him inside. It took everything within him to release her hand and let her go.

10

Linus did not take the news well.

Violet entered her family's sitting room with Owen's comforting presence behind her as her apparent intended paced back and forth in front of the chesterfield upon which her mother, father, and Daisy sat. Iris was sitting upon a chair across from them, a smirk on her face, while the Duke of Greenwich and Lord Westwood looked like handsome bookends as they leaned against each side of the hearth.

"You mean to tell me," Linus ranted, his arms waving in front of him, "That this inn has been used by soldiers for the past number of months, and because of your foolish decision, it is now in danger from the *French*?"

"Now see here, lad," Elias said, rising, "You are here because you are taking over the inn from *me*. You are not here to question my decisions, past or present. We have been well compensated by the Crown to house these men."

"Where has that money gone? And why, then, did you require funds from my father?" Linus questioned.

Dark crimson seeped into Elias' face. Violet bit her lip.

She had never questioned financial matters directly to her father, but she wondered herself where the income had gone.

"To improvements," Elias responded, and Linus looked about the room, his arms still flailing about him.

"Certainly not in these quarters. Why, this looks like the same furniture that was already outdated when I was a boy."

Violet's mother looked quite insulted, but her father raised a hand in front of her to still whatever words might emerge and answered Linus instead.

"Of course not. Improvements were in the guest quarters."

Anyone who had seen the guest quarters would know that not to be true, but now was not the time to enter into this conversation, though Violet didn't miss the look of disbelief that passed between her brothers-in-law, both who had resided there for a time.

"Very well. But now you tell me that things have gotten to the point in which we require a *militia*?"

"Oh, I wouldn't call it by such a formal name," Elias said. "A few men to protect the inn, just in case one disgruntled spy takes it upon himself to return here."

"My God," Linus said, looking stunned as he finally took a seat in the chair next to Iris.

Owen took that moment to make his presence known, as he stepped around Violet and more fully into the room

"I do hope you will join our mil— our effort," he said. "We meet daily in the mornings in the meadow just beyond the inn. The men each take a turn to act as a lookout at various posts."

Linus simply stared at him. "Who are you again?"

"Owen Ridlington. I fight for the English Crown, and I

am here to ensure the protection of The Wild Rose Inn and all of its inhabitants."

"I see," Linus said, though he made no promise to contribute to such protection. "I require a good meal and a good night's sleep to process all of this. When is dinner served? I will eat with the family."

"We eat after our guests are served," Daisy said, and Linus snorted.

"Very well. Tonight, then, I will eat with the guests."

Violet's line of vision was toward her brothers-in-law, and they looked as unimpressed with Linus as she was beginning to feel. She couldn't imagine what Owen thought of him. Here he was, a viscount who continually risked his life when he had no need to do so, while Linus couldn't bring himself to eat a late dinner, let alone join the other men who had willingly volunteered to protect what would soon be his.

Linus began to stride from the room when he noticed Violet standing there, just within the doorway. As his gaze fixed on her, Owen must have noted it too, for he tensed and his face froze in rigid dislike.

"Tavners," Linus said, addressing Violet's father, though he didn't turn from her. "Tomorrow, we should discuss our... arrangement, if you please."

"Very well," Elias said, though his voice was weary, and Violet shivered when Linus looked her up and down.

"Would you show me to my room, Violet?"

"Violet must prepare dinner," Iris interjected before Violet had a chance to reply. "I will show you."

Violet didn't think she had ever been more grateful to her sister, though she was somewhat surprised at her offer. Iris gave her a grim smile on her way out of the room. Clearly, she was not much enamored of Linus either. He hadn't been here long, but when Iris made up her mind about a person, it was difficult to change it. And she was seldom wrong.

As Linus stepped past her with one long final look, Violet couldn't help but compare him to Owen, who stood there stoically. Owen, who was willing to risk all for people he didn't know. Who gave up a life of leisure to serve his country. Who never seemed to waver from his beliefs or values in what was right and good.

And then Linus had come in here, questioning her father's actions, which were admirable, besides the fact that he likely had his own somewhat greedy motivations in mind.

Violet was no reader of people like Iris, but from what she had seen so far... could she really marry a man like Linus?

~

OWEN COULD HARDLY BELIEVE that Violet would even consider marrying the pest that was Linus Anderson. Surely, she must have more self-respect than to think she would have to resign herself with a man like him? Why, the first mention of any danger and he was ready to hide in his room until the threat was gone.

But if this inn was truly what she wanted in life, if this was what she imagined true happiness to be... then so be it.

Owen lay down on the sagging mattress that was really the only furniture in the room aside from the washbasin and dresser of drawers that had seen better days. The room was certainly clean and serviceable, but he could tell first-hand that no investment into it had been made for some time.

Not that he minded. While he had slept in much better conditions, he had also slept in much worse.

Ah, Violet. He sighed. Pretty, whimsical, Violet. He had thought she would be a romantic, with all of her notions from her books, but damn Comtois had robbed her of those dreams for her own self.

Now he had a decision to make. Did he attempt to restore those dreams to her head, filling the role of hero? For he didn't know what sort of hero he would make. He could very well be an absentee husband who could never give her the attention she deserved.

He sighed. For now, this was not something he had the time to question. While he didn't want to put anyone in any further jeopardy, he secretly wished that Comtois would come here and attempt an attack on the inn, for if he could capture him once more then he could put this entire business behind him. And then he would make his decision — woo Violet, or leave The Wild Rose Inn in Southwold and never return.

∾

"PISTOLS UP! Aim! Fire! That's it, very good, men, very good."

Violet watched Owen's militia from a shaded spot at the edge of the meadow, a place where she was hidden from view of them all — most especially Owen. She had no wish to either get in their way or for him to know that she was watching him. She simply couldn't help herself. She hadn't spent any time at all with him over the past few days. They had barely even spoken, unless one counted his "Thank you" when she served him dinner. Hardly the most romantic words one ever heard, and they certainly would never be found on the pages of any of her novels.

She wasn't sure what she was supposed to do, though. Tell Owen that she couldn't even think about Linus when her feelings for him ran much deeper than she could have imagined? He had kissed her, true, but perhaps it had just been a moment between the two of them, one that didn't extend past soft-spoken words in the beauty that had surrounded them.

"Vi?"

Violet jumped when Iris called her name and turned to see her approaching from the path that connected the inn with the meadow.

She hoped her sister would assume she was just passing by.

But Iris was more astute than that.

"You are watching your Mr. Ridlington?"

"No, of course not," Violet said, her face warming. "I was interested in seeing what they were doing out here, that's all."

"Mmm-hmm," Iris said with a grin, and Violet sighed.

"I'm not sure what to think, Iris," she confessed, and Iris tilted her head as her smile faded and she regarded her sister with much more seriousness. "I thought that, perhaps, there was something there, but even if Owen—that is, Mr. Ridlington—does feel something toward me, clearly everything else that is occurring is much more important."

"Maybe it is important to him *because* he is protecting you," Iris pointed out, and Violet looked down at her hands.

"Perhaps. But I think this is what drives him — the ability to fight for others in whatever way he can, no matter who they are."

Iris bit her lip. "He spends all day training, then goes on watch until another relieves him," she said. "The man hardly has time to eat and sleep."

"I know."

"Yet still, one cannot help but want to be acknowledged by the man she loves."

Violet looked up at her sharply, seeing the amusement in Iris' crystal blue eyes. "I do not love him!"

"Do you not?" Iris questioned, raising one of her shapely eyebrows. "It is not as though your head is never in the clouds, Violet, but the past few days you have hardly opened your mouth to respond to anything anyone says to you. Why, you've been walking around in a daze, and yet I have hardly seen a book in your hands. I believe it is because you are in the midst of your own love story, with your Mr. Ridlington."

Violet cringed. "Perhaps you have some of it right, but the story, I believe, would be one of my own making. Oh, Iris, I hardly know what to think any longer!"

"Well I know one thing," Iris said. "You simply *must* tell Father that you want nothing more to do with Linus Anderson. I don't think I've ever met a more horrid man!" She paused for a moment. "Well, perhaps Ernest Abernathy. But Linus may be far more annoying. I still have not forgiven him for spooking your horse all those years ago. My goodness, Violet, you cannot actually be considering spending your life with such a man!"

"He is not that terrible..."

"He truly is."

Violet sighed. "I suppose you are right. I tried to talk to Father about it once already, but he told me that the deal is basically complete. It seems he wasn't quite aware of just how adamant Linus was that the hotel came with a bride."

"Listen to what you are saying, Violet," Iris admonished her. "That it *comes* with a *bride*! You will be nothing more than a servant to the man. A servant who must go to his bed! No, Violet, absolutely not."

"I just don't know how to say no to him, and to Father, now that all has been arranged. Our parents have done so much for us, Iris, that I must at least consider this possibility."

"They raised us, Violet, just as any parent should," Iris argued. "They fed us and clothed us, gave us a roof over our heads, true. But we basically worked for it. We've spent our lives slaving at this inn."

"Working for our parents, as do most children," Violet countered, and Iris sighed, placing her hands on her hips.

"You are a much better person than I, Violet, to be so giving. You always see the best in others. But you have also always had the most romantic heart I've ever known. You dream of more, Vi. Allow those dreams to come true. Do not settle."

Violet took one more long look across the meadow at Owen. She seemed to be able to find him in moments, despite the fact that the meadow was dotted with men.

Her heart had known the truth long before her head. She loved him. She loved him for his bravery, for his compassion, and for his instinct to put others before himself.

Now, what was she going to do about it?

11

O wen knew he should just leave the situation be. Linus Anderson and the inn were really none of his business. But he just couldn't keep himself from having a bit of fun at the man's expense — and, if he were being honest with himself, he did have a few ulterior motives. He had spotted Violet watching their practice earlier that day but hadn't said anything. Truth be told, he wasn't exactly sure what to say. Until he knew whether or not there was any future for them, he had to stay away or he wouldn't be able to keep his hands off of her. But that didn't mean he had to like the fact that there was another vying for her affections.

"Anderson!" Owen called as he entered the family dining room and saw the man's retreating back. Anderson continued to insist that he was part of the family and not one of the guests.

The man reactively looked back before obviously thinking better of the action and attempted to pretend he hadn't heard Owen. But with a few long strides Owen caught up to him, and Anderson had no choice but to turn to him.

"Ah, Ridlington. How are you today? Busy with your little soldiers?"

Owen raised his eyebrows.

"My *little soldiers* are coming along just fine. And, in fact, we would be pleased for you to join us if you'd like. I'm still awaiting your response."

"Ah, ha..." Anderson said, his eyes flitting from one side of the corridor to the other. "As much as I would enjoy partaking, I find myself otherwise occupied. As a matter of fact, since we are now speaking anyway, there is something of which I would like to talk to you about."

"Very well," Owen said, crossing his arms over his chest. This should be interesting.

"It seems to me that the very threat to this inn, and this town for that matter, is due to the soldiers who are currently making their home here. Would not the best solution to this threat be for you all to simply leave?"

Although he bristled at the man's suggestion, Owen had already thought of this himself. It was not, however, his decision to make, and besides, he felt it was too late now to diminish any potential threat.

"Comtois would not know that we are no longer here, and therefore the inn would be left defenseless," he said and had to bite his cheek to keep from smiling when he saw how Anderson paled at the words as he realized that he would be left here without anyone to fight for him. "You wouldn't want that, now would you?"

"Of course I would not want... the women here left alone," he said. "As for myself, I am unsure of just how long I will be staying at this particular time. I had hoped to be married and assuming my duties immediately, but apparently, there has been a bit of a misunderstanding."

"Oh?" Owen asked, attempting to appear disinterested.

"Yes, the bride is not quite as willing as I had thought she would be. She'll come around, however."

"She will, will she?"

"Yes, of course. Her father has promised to have a stern discussion with her on this very day. Then I will take her for a walk, charm her a little, and all will be well. Why, you may even be here for the wedding."

Owen managed a grim smile, realizing by Anderson's own sly grin that he seemed to be more aware of Owen's feelings toward Violet than he would have wished.

"Well, I wish you the best of luck," he said as he took his leave, unable to stand another moment of this conversation. Anderson had proven himself to be the coward Owen had suspected.

"Violet!" he heard Elias Tavners shout from down the corridor. "I must speak with you."

Violet emerged from the kitchen, stopping suddenly when she saw Owen. Her hair was pulled back from her face, a scarf around it, her cheeks pink with warmth from the kitchen. Her work dress was made of a stiff, ugly fabric, and yet nothing could diminish the beauty that radiated from her.

Suddenly he wanted nothing more than to run to her, pick her up and take her from here to his home, where she would have others doing such work for her, where she wouldn't have to worry about cooking, cleaning, making beds, or hiding from French spies.

Well, she may still have that last worry.

She stared at him, her eyes speaking the volumes that her words did not.

"Owen," she began. "I—"

"Violet!"

"I must speak with my father," she said, her expression turning into steely resolve, and then she turned and followed Tavners into his study.

Knowing what this conversation was about, Owen had an urge to run in, slam the door behind him, and tell Elias Tavners in no uncertain terms that he, the Viscount of Primrose, was going to marry his daughter no matter what other agreement had been made.

But this must be Violet's decision. Then, he had his own to make.

One thing he did know — he was nearly finished with The Wild Rose Inn and the men who portended to care for it. He'd see this through and then be gone.

Whether or not Violet would be with him remained to be seen.

∼

"VIOLET, COME IN, COME IN," her father said, all jovial spirits as he waved to the ripped chair in front of his desk.

"Father," she said before he could speak. "I know what this is about."

He reddened. "I'm not sure—"

"Is it about Linus Anderson, marriage, and this inn?"

"Ahh— yes."

"Right. Well, I have come to a decision about all of this."

"Well, that's the thing, Violet," he said, wringing his hands together now in front of him. "When we initially spoke of this, I was under the impression that you would have more opportunity to make a decision than I first thought. It seems that Linus, the dear boy, is so infatuated with you..." he gave an uneasy chuckle. "...that he simply *must* have you as his wife."

She gaped in silence.

He offered another breathy laugh, beads of sweat appearing on his brow. "Now if that isn't true young love, I don't know what is."

Violet stood and leaned over, placing her hands on her father's desk in a display of emotion that seemed to shock him, for she was never one to do so. Iris, yes, but Violet...

"I do not care what *you* agreed to, Father," she said vehemently, all of the pent-up emotion that had been filling inside of her now overflowing. "All I agreed to was to *meet* Linus and spend time with him to determine if this was what I wanted. And I must tell you, things have changed. I do *not* wish to marry him and stay here at the inn. I know that is what you wanted, Father, and I am sorry to disappoint you, but it simply cannot be. He is arrogant and presumptuous, and I have spent much of my life working as hard as I can to make this inn prosperous, and at the very least, I would like to be with a man who would *help* me to do so, not work me like a slave."

She took a deep breath, noting when she did so that her father's jaw had gone slack, his mouth open in shock that she would speak to him in such a way. She knew she had likely crossed the line, that there was no going back now, but it seemed that since she had opened her mouth, she couldn't stop the flow of words that emerged from it.

"For all of our lives we — all four of us — have done your bidding. I know that is what is expected of us, but Father, you have done nothing to make this inn any better than what it is. Maybe if you took some of the earnings and truly put them into improving this place then we could charge more, and you could make more and hire another maid or two in our place and then you wouldn't have to marry me off. But no, instead you gamble it all away and then beg your daughters' husbands for more!"

Violet was breathing heavily now, her hands on her hips as she stared at her father. Now that she had said all that she wanted to, guilt and fear tempered her anger. She had gone far past where she should have stopped. She stood, waiting for her father to bellow at her, to tell her to get out of his study, to leave the inn and to never return.

But he just sat there, staring at her. His jaw worked a couple of times beneath his gray beard, but no sound came out.

Finally, she said softly. "I will just leave, then," and he held up a hand to stop her.

This time when his mouth opened, he managed a few words. "Violet," he said, his voice just above a whisper. "I'm sorry."

"Pardon me?" she asked, incredulity overcoming all else.

"I'm sorry," he said a little louder this time as he ran a hand over his face and his hair. "You are right."

He looked down at his desk as though he was unable to lift his gaze to her. "I have failed you. I failed you all. It was just... once I lost some money down at my card games, I couldn't stop. I kept thinking, I'll play again and make it back. If I bet once more, I can overcome my losses. And then I win and I think, I can do so again. But..." He shook his head. "I'll speak to Linus. I'll tell him we must renegotiate our deal. I'm sure he will understand."

Violet wasn't so sure about that, but at least she wouldn't end up married to the man.

"Thank you, Father," she said, sitting down once more and reaching across the table to take his hand. "I appreciate it. And I'm sorry... for some of the things I said."

"It was the truth," he admitted. "I suppose I have some planning to do now. Your mother and I will not be able to keep up with this place forever, and I did make a deal with George."

Another wave of guilt assaulted her, but Violet thought on all that Iris had said to her. She couldn't give up her whole life. She would find another way to care for her parents. For goodness sake, her sisters were married to noblemen. They could determine some solution.

"I'd best go finish supper," she said when she noticed her hands were shaking, and she made for the door before tears began to slide down her face.

She opened the door to see Iris scurrying down the hall, which caused a laugh to overcome her sorrowful feelings.

"Iris!" she called, and her sister turned, biting her lip.

"You caught me."

"You never change," Violet said, shaking her head.

"Well, I'm afraid I couldn't hear much, what with the keyhole being blocked and all," Iris said sheepishly. "But from what I heard... oh Violet, you stood up to Father. I cannot tell you how proud I am."

Violet shook her head.

"I went too far, said too much—"

"I think you said what you needed to for him to listen," Iris said. "And thank you for doing so. You did what the rest of us should have ages ago. Now," she leaned in conspiratorially, "Does this mean that you will be declaring your love for your Mr. Ridlington?"

Violet was filled with nerves anew.

"I have no idea if he feels the same. He has hardly looked my way in days."

"Maybe that's because he thinks you are going to marry

83

Linus Anderson," Iris said, rolling her eyes. "Just talk to him, Vi. I have a feeling he'll surprise you."

"Very well," Violet said, clenching her hands together to stop their shaking. "Owen Ridlington," she muttered, "I'm coming for you."

12

Owen was surprised to find a message had arrived for him that evening. He had been eager — and yet equally apprehensive — about finding time to be alone with Violet, to learn more of her conversation with her father. Had she chosen Linus Anderson and the inn, or was she going to pursue more for herself?

If she did... well, he had a few things he would like to say to her. Promises, perhaps. At the very least, he was beginning to feel that he had to tell her exactly what he thought of her, and then allow her to make her decision. He glanced down at the note in his hands.

LORD PRIMROSE,

WE HAVE no leads on Comtois at this time, so I require you to remain in Southwold. I apologize that we cannot spare any additional men to aid you.

I write with some unsettling news. I regret to inform you that *last night, there was an attack on your estate. There was hardly a soul about, but your butler suffered injuries when the men forced their way in. Nothing was stolen, for it seems they were looking for you.*

There is no need to return, but I would suggest that you remain on diligent watch, though I have no doubt that if there was ever a man who could look out for himself, it would be you.

I will be in touch when I have more to report. I hope that this will come to a quick conclusion, as there are other matters with which we require your assistance.

GENERAL DOBBINS

THE PAPER FELL out of Owen's hands and fluttered to the floor. An attack on his home. He had been involved in many situations that had threatened his life, but never before had his home been violated. This was personal, and it called into question everything he knew to be true, including his own future and what it might hold. He could not very well offer Violet anything — even a promise — if it meant that her life might be in danger. Once Comtois was caught, she would be far safer here, without Owen.

He sat down on the settee in the sitting room, removed his hat, and ran a hand through his hair as an ache began deep in his chest and spread through his body, to the point where he thought he would be sick.

A life without Violet... never would he have thought it would hurt so much to imagine it. And now that it was a reality, it felt as though it was going to break him. He had thought he was a stronger man than that, but love, apparently, brought a man to his knees. And he didn't like it. Not one bit.

~

VIOLET WAS UPSTAIRS PREPARING for bed when she looked out her window and saw Owen standing on the shore, looking out at the ocean. Her heart felt as though it skipped a beat as she gazed upon his lean, strong profile. The pull to go to him was nearly impossible to ignore, and she thought on all that had occurred today. She had stood up to her father, had said no to Linus, and had never felt such relief before.

Now it was time to speak her truth, to tell Owen how she really felt. If she didn't, she would regret it for the rest of her life. Perhaps he felt nothing of the same for her. What she would then do with her future, she had no idea. But she had to try.

Violet turned and looked at herself in the mirror. She hadn't yet changed out of her pale pink muslin dress, but she had let down her hair. She should put it back together before greeting Owen, but by then it might be too late — he could be gone.

For once in her life, she decided it was time to take a risk, and she was out the door and down the stairs before she could change her mind.

Violet wasn't sure whether she was excited or simply anxious as she stood at the edge of the beach, looking at Owen as he gazed out over the water. Most would wonder what he was looking at, but Violet knew better. She spent many a moment staring out at nothing, while her head filled with images that were far more exciting. Of what he was

ELLIE ST. CLAIR

thinking, she had no idea, but she hoped that he might share some of that — and more — with her.

"Owen?" she called softly as she approached, and he quickly turned on his heel at her voice. His face was pinched and pensive, far from its usual easy careless expression.

"Violet," he murmured, the warmth in his voice coursing through her in waves. Goodness, he was handsome. It still seemed to take her by surprise every time she looked at him. She gazed at his lips, visible through his dark beard, and imagined herself kissing them once more. But then she shook her head. This was the time for words, not action.

"I must speak with you," she began, but he lifted a hand.

"Would you mind if I share something with you first?"

"I... I suppose," she said, her elation at telling him all that had happened falling slightly as she awaited his words, but if he was going to tell her how he felt, that... perhaps, he loved her? Could it be? Then she was willing to wait. Except his expression was rather stoic and not at all tender.

"Violet, I think that you should marry Linus and stay here at the inn."

Violet's heart stopped. Or, at least, it felt as though it did, for the rest of the world continued to move about her, even though everything she had known to be true seemed to suddenly change.

"Can you say that again?" she asked in a small voice.

He took a step closer to her, so that they were only a foot or so apart, though it seemed like a mile now stretched between them.

"I know you have been struggling with the decision of what to do with your life. And I know that your father wants this for you. I haven't said anything to you before now

88

because I felt that you should make this decision on your own. But now..."

"Now what?" she asked, hearing her voice hard and bitter, but she couldn't help herself. *Now* he decided to have something to say to her?

He looked down at the ground between them, his hands on his hips, before he raised his head up to take her in once more.

"I have greatly enjoyed our time together," he said, and she could only stare at him as his words rang through her.

She should have known. She was nothing more than a distraction until a greater purpose came along.

"But I realize now that nothing more can come of this — whatever it is — between us. I have nothing to offer you. My life is one mission after another, and who is to say for how long that will continue? I have made enemies and while the inn is not, at the moment, a place of safety, it will be again. You know what to expect from a life here. You love this place. You have your gardens, your books, your friends. If we... if we were to ever progress beyond our time together here, you might be put in danger from those out for revenge against me. I cannot do that to you."

As he spoke, his words brought both relief and fear. Relief that it wasn't, perhaps, the fact that he didn't feel anything for her, but rather that he still put his role of protector above all else. And fear due to the resolve in his voice, for he was a man who would not be deterred when he was sure of something, especially when it meant keeping another safe.

"Many take me to be meek and mild," she said, finding her voice, forcing herself to say what was in her heart. What did it matter? He would be gone from here soon anyway, so she may as well say what she had come here to tell him.

"But that is not necessarily the case. It is just that my sisters — well, mostly Iris — always seem to be saying enough. But when something matters, I feel it is best to say what is on my mind. And in this case, well, it matters." She paused. "I said no to my father. I actually said much more than that, but that is beside the point. I said no to marrying Linus, to spending the rest of my life at The Wild Rose Inn. I love this place, but this is not what I want for myself. Especially if it means spending my life with Linus. I had resigned myself to the fact that I would never find love — true love — but I was wrong."

She finally worked up the courage to look into his eyes, and what she read there was not the hope that she would have liked to have seen, but rather pain.

"Violet—"

"I love you, Owen Ridlington. You are a man who puts others before yourself, who doesn't take what was handed to him but has formed a life that has meaning. I think I admire you more than I've ever admired another, and I would like nothing more than to spend my life with you. Even though you haven't offered it, and now," her voice broke, "it seems as though you likely never will."

She took a step backward, ready to run. She had said what she came here to say, but now she knew that there would be no reciprocation. Owen opened his mouth as though to say something, and she cringed, waiting for his rejection. But then he suddenly stepped forward, filling the gap she had created between them, and brought his mouth down upon hers, kissing her hard, possessively, as though telling her with his actions exactly what he felt he couldn't with his words. One hand came behind her head, his fingers twining into her unbound hair. Suddenly she was quite pleased that she hadn't taken an extra moment to put it back up again.

His lips roved over hers with more passion than she ever could have asked for, and yet... this was not a kiss of promise. As he broke away and stared down at her with glazed eyes, she knew what this was, and it filled her with sorrow. This was a kiss of goodbye.

"Violet..." he said, his voice raspy, and she shook her head. She didn't want to hear it.

"Violet, I'm sorry," he began again, but she raised her hand in front of her, warning him off as she backed away. She willed her tears to remain inside, but she couldn't help when a few squeezed out of her eyes anyway and rolled down her cheeks.

"Violet, please, I... I just have nothing I can say, I can't—"

But this time, she didn't let him finish. She turned on her heel and raced away as quickly as she could, so she wouldn't have to face him any longer.

13

———————

"I just don't know what is left for me."

Violet couldn't see them from her stance near the window, but she could practically feel her sisters' looks of pity on her back. It had been two long days since Owen had told her that there was no future to be had between the two of them. Two days of avoiding his eyes when she had to serve him, of hiding her tears, splashing water on her puffy cheeks, and attempting to go about her day as if nothing was wrong — as if her whole world hadn't fallen apart.

"You are young still, Vi," Daisy said gently, placing a hand on her back. "You don't know what could be awaiting you."

"If Linus takes the inn—" she cringed at the thought, "— then where does that leave me? He has promised Mother and Father a small cottage and stipend in exchange for the inn, but what would I do with myself?"

"Mother and Father will never turn you out," Daisy said, though her voice lacked conviction and Violet could have sworn she heard Iris snort.

"Father has asked that, even if I will not marry Linus, I help him run the inn for a time," Violet said, her voice bitter. "Apparently Linus is convinced that he cannot do it alone."

"Oh Vi, you simply cannot do such a thing," Iris said vehemently. "You would be ruined — scandalized — if you lived here alone with the man. Why, it is nothing more than a ploy to force you into marriage, and Father shouldn't be so stupid that he doesn't realize it."

"You see?" Violet said morosely. "No options."

"What do they call this moment in your books, Vi?" Daisy asked, and Violet could hear her attempting optimism. "The storm before the rainbow? Things will get better. They must."

Violet leaned her forehead against the cool glass as she looked out over the ocean below, while her sisters sat on the bed behind her.

"I thought I felt something for Comtois but look how that turned out. Now I fall in love — truly fall in love — and the man tells me that there is no future for the two of us. I am living a tragedy, not a romance."

She knew she was being as dramatic as Iris, but she couldn't help herself.

"He may come around," Iris said with an attempt at enthusiasm, but Violet shook her head.

"He was fairly resolute."

All was silent for a moment as her sisters had clearly run out of anything remotely optimistic to say.

"You will come live with me," Daisy said suddenly, causing Violet to turn from the window.

"Pardon me?"

"I said, you will come live with me," Daisy said with conviction. "I have a massive home in London and an even bigger one in the country. Both are filled with the most beautiful rooms, more numerous than those here in the inn, and all of them are sitting empty. Nathaniel would be happy to have you, as would his mother and sister. They enjoy all sorts of events. You would love the theatre, Violet, and in London, there is access to the most amazing circulation libraries and bookstores — it would be perfect."

Violet managed a small smile for her sister.

"I cannot live off your charity."

"Not forever," Daisy said with a shrug. "Simply long enough for you to come to find a man of your own or a calling you enjoy. I know it feels like you may never love again, but you never know, Vi. There are plenty of men in London, and one might catch your eye."

Daisy was trying so hard that Violet couldn't help but give her a slight nod in order to appease her, but she knew, deep within her soul, the truth of the matter.

She would never love again.

～

OWEN RAN a weary hand over his face as he re-entered the inn that night. After training the militia that morning, he had spent the rest of the day on watch before handing off his duty to another.

He had to admit that he had not been the best of commanders these days, for all he could think of was Violet.

Violet, with eyes true to her name, a heart of gold, and a whimsical air that seemed to have been lost after they had last spoken. He was as bad as Comtois for taking from her the romantic spirit that had always followed her around, and he hated himself for it.

But it was for the best, he told himself for the hundredth time that day. She was safer and would be happier here.

After eating a quick meal of leftover roast pork and potatoes, he pushed back from the table and trudged up the stairs to his room, which had never looked more barren nor bleaker.

Similar to his future.

He kicked off his boots and lay down, praying he would quickly fall asleep.

God was being merciful, for he did.

It seemed like moments later but was in actuality a few hours when a scream abruptly woke Owen. He looked around wildly as he attempted to determine from where it was coming, but it was rooms away. He bolted to his feet, forcing them back into his boots before he threw open the door to his room and began running down the corridor.

And that's when he smelled it. Smoke.

He couldn't see it yet, nor were flames apparent, but there would be a source, and it must be close.

Owen began to knock on the door of every room he passed, waking the soldiers who slept within, if they had not already risen. "Up, up!" he called as he raced through the building and out the front door, where he saw others from the town had begun to congregate.

"The fire's in the back!" someone called, and Owen nodded. He had trained a militia, and while their mock opponents had never been fire, his men were nonetheless prepared to fight.

"Is there a fire brigade?" he called, but there was no one near enough with knowledge of the town to answer — only former soldiers who resided at the inn now looking at him with expressions as confused as his own. "To the kitchens," he called. "Look for buckets!"

"That's where the fire started, Ridlington!"

Bollocks. They were near a water source at the very least.

He ran to the road to see if anyone had started fighting this fire, and was relieved to see men from the town pushing a wood pumper toward the inn.

"Thank God," he said, running to meet it, finding the blacksmith and his son-in-law, who seemed to be leading the charge of the men at the helm.

"Does this thing work?" Owen asked, and the blacksmith shrugged.

"It should," he said. "Hasn't been used in a time, though. And our brigade... well, it's more of a list of men, and most are part of your militia. They respond well to you, so I'll leave them in your hands." He turned back and looked at Owen once more. "You do know how to fight a fire, do you not?"

He didn't really, but this was no time to question himself. "Have you buckets?"

"Underneath."

Owen nodded then began shouting to the men who had emerged from the inn and were congregating on the grass beyond the building.

"Form a line from the shore!" he said, then began to organize them as best he could before turning back to look at the inn. The kitchens were ablaze now, and the flames looked to be threatening the family quarters.

"Violet," he said under his breath, and then took off at a run. "Violet!" he shouted now, looking wildly around him as he searched out the Tavners family.

Someone gripped his arm, and he turned, hoping to see a pair of violet eyes staring back at him, but instead it was the strong gaze of Nathaniel Huntingwell.

"I'll gather the family," he said, and Owen nodded his thanks, though his heart was wherever Violet was.

He wanted to run into the inn and look for her, but he

knew she was likely already outside and he could do the most good out here, directing the men, to hopefully try to save this inn.

He ran to the wood pumper, where the blacksmith was taking some of the buckets from the last man in the line and pouring them into the lead-lined trough in the main part of the equipment. He called to the second man — Burt, his name was — to start pumping the arms, and when he did, water shot out of the apparatus in a steady stream.

"Good job, men!" Owen called, but when he looked at the inn, he could see that the kitchens, where the pumper was being aimed, were already lost. "Point it to the family quarters!" he said, hoping that they could save those rooms where the flames were beginning to threaten. He directed those with buckets to focus on the same area.

Where, oh where, was Violet? He saw Daisy and Iris standing to the side with their parents, Linus Anderson, and a small blond woman watching the firefighting efforts with looks of horror upon their faces.

"Westwood!" he called out to the man who was leaving the family to begin helping with the effort. "Where is Violet?"

"I'm not sure," Westwood yelled back, his voice barely carrying over the shouts of the other men and the crackle of the fire. People from the town had begun to gather, watching the fight. "Greenwich is in there looking for her."

As Westwood mentioned him, the man ran from the inn, looking wildly around him.

"Has she emerged?" asked Greenwich through a paroxysm of coughing.

"No!" Westwood shouted, and Owen's heart began to beat faster than it ever had before. Just then, he heard a cry and saw that the other side of the inn, near the guest entrance, had caught fire as well. What in the... it was as though this fire was being deliberately started. Suddenly a growing fear worked its way through his body. No. No, no, no. Comtois.

He took off toward the building, even as questions were called out to him from the men as to where exactly they should be focusing.

"Greenwich," he called to the Duke, "Take over!"

He nodded, understanding dawning on his face as Owen ran into the inn.

"Violet!" Owen called, but hearing nothing, he tried again. "Violet!" He coughed as the smoke engulfed him, choking the air from his lungs, and he fell to his knees to try to avoid it as he began to crawl past the family dining room.

He inched down the hallway, calling Violet's name over and over again, but not hearing anything. He questioned whether he should venture up to the second floor, but he had no idea which was her chamber and he assumed her family or Greenwich would have already looked there for her.

Suddenly a thought dawned on him. The gardens. She often sat in a corner that would be hidden from the beach and the meadow, which was near the kitchen and the dining room. The smoke would be nearly as thick there as inside the building itself due to the way the walls formed a courtyard of sorts.

He forced his way outdoors and saw a form sitting just where he would have pictured her on a regular day, reading her book.

"Violet!" he stood now, rushing forward to her, in equal measure relieved to have found her and yet also deeply scared as to her condition. Her head was lolling down upon her chest, and she was limp in a chair — a chair to which she was... tied? What in the....

"My God, Violet," he said, lifting his shirt to hold it over his face as he worked at the ties that bound her. Luckily, the ropes came free rather quickly, and he lifted her in his arms, wrapping them tightly around her as he raced out of the enclosed space, where debris was beginning to rain down around them.

Owen had never been one who spoke often to God, but at this moment, he prayed with all his might that Violet was alive and that she would be fine. Please, God, let her be fine. He ran to the beach, where the air seemed fresh and clear in comparison to the inn and its gardens. He looked back now, seeing that the makeshift brigade was actually doing a decent job of fighting the fire, and perhaps — just perhaps — some of the inn might be saved.

He laid Violet down on the grass, running his hands over her as he attempted to wake her up.

"Violet!" he cried. "Please, Violet, look at me!"

He leaned down to find her breath, and upon seeing her chest moving ever so softly up and down, he breathed a sigh of relief.

"Thank God."

Her sisters came to join him now, and he sat back on his heels, closing his eyes. There was moisture on his cheeks, and he had no idea if the tears were a result of the smoke or his own desperation.

Her eyelids fluttered ever so slightly, and she reached up a hand to him. He grasped it, holding it against his face, reveling in the life-force that accompanied it.

Her lips formed an "O" but when she tried to speak, her words only came out as a gasp, and a few weak coughs. She had breathed a lot of smoke.

"Don't say anything," he said, gripping her hand tighter. "We'll find a physician."

She shook her head and then pointed toward the building, her eyes open now, desperately seeking his as she sought to tell him something.

He turned now, following her finger, and as he did, he thought he saw a spark on the side of the building. His focus returned to the fact that the fire had been started in multiple locations. It was set deliberately, and Violet was the one targeted. Comtois was still here.

Owen looked between the building and Violet, torn between the need to stay with her and the urge to race after Comtois.

"Go," Daisy urged, crouching down beside her sister, and Iris nodded. Looking between them, realizing Violet would be safe, he backed away, but not before turning to Westwood.

"Watch over them," he ordered the man, and after Westwood nodded resolutely, Owen took off after Comtois.

14

Owen entered the trees as silently as possible, though stealth was hardly necessary, due to the crackling of the fire in the building above him. Much of it was built of brick and stone, so would hopefully survive, but everything within it would likely be reduced to ashes. At least all were safe; that was what mattered.

That and catching the man responsible.

Owen rounded the corner where it seemed a fire had most recently been started, and as he inched around the side of the inn that was adjacent to the stables, he spotted his quarry. He looked decidedly more disheveled than at their last meeting, but Owen supposed that was what happened following imprisonment. Upon his escape, he would have had little opportunity to clean himself, and the clothes he wore looked stolen, for they were decidedly too small. But that didn't keep the evil smirk from his face as he used a lantern to set a piece of cloth on fire before holding it up as though to throw it upon the building.

"Comtois!" Owen called to stop him, and the man turned quickly to his voice. When he saw Owen, however, he did not look dismayed but rather grinned so wickedly that Owen shuddered.

"Ah, Owen Ridlington. Or, should I say, *Seigneur* Primrose." He laughed. "I see I have shocked you. *Oui*, I know who you are. Just as I know that you are enamored with the Tavners girl. Did you find my little gift? I had actually hoped it would take you longer and the two of you would perish together. How romantic would that be?"

Owen narrowed his eyes at him. He had no wish to engage in verbal barbs with the man. He would far rather come to physical blows, but that would have to wait. He wished he had a weapon on him, but he had left his hands free in favor of carrying buckets. Some of the men had been wielding axes to help fight the fire, and now he wished he had picked one up himself.

However, this was partly providential, for there was one thing he needed to know.

"Where are the rest of them?"

"The rest of what?"

"Your allies."

A look flashed in Comtois' eyes, one that was quite telling. The man was alone, though he attempted to convince Owen otherwise.

"They will be coming upon you shortly, Primrose. I would far prefer to finish you myself, however. You and the dastardly Westwood." Comtois frowned. "This is not going according to plan, you know. The lot of you were supposed to be encased in the inn right now as it burned to the ground, but the fire within the garden never caught. You had a touch of luck today, *mon ami*. Until now, that is."

It was then that Owen saw the pistol in Comtois' hand as it twitched at his side. Owen inched ever closer. If he could reach him, then he could knock it out of his hand and the two of them could engage in hand-to-hand combat. That, he knew he could win.

"Why didn't you return to France?" he asked, buying time.

"I had to complete my business here first," Comtois said, raising the pistol and leveling it at him.

Don't shoot, Owen thought. *I need a minute. One minute more. And then I can wrest the pistol away, go back to Violet, tell her that I love her and want to spend our lives together.*

Comtois' finger tightened on the trigger, and life passed before Owen — not his past, however, but his future. The future that he would never have if that bullet hit him in the right place.

If I survive this, he promised, *I'll do everything right. I'll look after Violet, give up everything else, and commit myself to her.*

He cringed as Comtois narrowed his eyes and began to squeeze the trigger. A large "crack" announced the firing of the gun. Owen waited for the bullet to hit, noting that time truly did slow down when in moments such as this.

A wave of heat rolled over him.

But the bullet never came.

He looked up to find Comtois had vanished. In his place was a section of the inn that had fallen from the second story, landing on top of the man. The glare of the fire made Owen squint his eyes as he shied from the hot flames. That must have been what had caused the crack, and the reason the bullet had never fired.

Owen knew he should run before the rest of the building fell, but first he had to make sure that this was the last they would see of the French spy. He inched closer, careful as he picked his way through the debris, and finally saw Comtois' boot sticking out from below a pile of bricks. He attempted to pull some of them off of him, but the mangled body beneath was not something which he wanted to spend much time over.

Comtois was dead, and would never be a threat to them again.

The moment the relief began to wash over him, he wasted not another moment before running clear of the building and any potential threat. He had much to live for now and was not going to fall victim to this inn.

Noting the newly formed fire brigade seemed to have everything well in hand, his heart led him back to where he had last left Violet. She was now sitting up, her family attending to her. They stepped back, parting to allow him to walk to her. He bent down on one knee and lifted her hands in his.

"Violet," he said softly, looking into her eyes, grateful to find that her returned gaze was steady and even.

"Owen," she said, her voice still guttural but much clearer now.

"I thought I'd lost you," he said, hearing his voice break but no longer caring. In the back of his mind, he noted that her family had stepped backward — though Daisy had to pull Iris away — to allow them a moment alone. He intended to take full advantage.

He reached out and cupped her cheek, the ashes on his hand mixing with those upon her face.

"I'm stronger than you think," she said with a small smile, and he nodded, knowing that her words had never been truer. Even as she sat there with her hair strewn about her, soot upon her cheeks, her nightgown torn and bedraggled, she was the most beautiful thing he had ever seen.

He couldn't stop the words before they poured out of his mouth.

"I love you, Violet Tavners."

~

VIOLET LOOKED up at Owen in shock. Had he truly just said those words to her? And did he actually mean them or was it simply due to the excitement of the moment?

Her mind was still slightly hazy but his face was as clear as could be as he knelt down in front of her, his warm, calloused hands still encasing hers as his thumbs massaged the backs of her hands.

"You don't have to say that, Owen," she said, shaking her head before she could allow hope to invade her soul. "I understand—"

"No, you don't," he said with more urgency. "Not if you don't believe me. I've been a fool, Violet."

"You could never be a fool."

"But I have."

He paused, looking down for a moment, and seeing the struggle within him, she patiently waited for him to continue, doing all she could to not allow her emotions to get the better of her, but to wait and see what it was he had to say.

"I thought..." He cleared his throat. "I thought that by keeping you away from me I was keeping you safe. That by distancing myself, not allowing a future together, you would have a far better chance at happiness. But I realize now that safety is never guaranteed. That I will always love you, no matter where I am or where you are. Perhaps the very best way to keep you safe — and to make you happy — is to be with you. If you'll have me, that is."

Of course she would have him! Her heart was nearly

ELLIE ST. CLAIR

bursting to exclaim such a thing, but he apparently had more to say.

"I don't know what kind of life I can offer you," Owen said. "I can never fully commit my time to you and my home until we've defeated Napoleon and his forces. You may have to live elsewhere while I'm away to ensure your own safety. It's not much of a life, I'm afraid, and I hate asking you to wait, Violet, but wait you may have to do until this war is finished."

She bit her lip, considering the fact that after what they had been through, she could still lose him in whatever battles remained. The alternative, however, was losing him and his love regardless.

"What I can promise you," he continued, "is that I will do all I can to remain with you, to love with all of myself when I am with you. I will give you as much of the world as possible, Violet. I will take you places that you have only read about in your books. I will build you a library worthy of a queen. If that's not enough... I do understand. But I needed you to know how I feel."

"Oh, Owen," she said, tears beginning to form, and he sat her up, placing an arm behind her back so that their faces were even. "I don't need any of that. All I need is for you to love me even half as much as I love you."

He looked at her for a moment, his face filled with disbelief as a wide grin began to form, ever so slowly, until it broke out across his face.

"We may be having a battle here, Violet," he said, and she raised an eyebrow, "as I would argue that I love *you* more."

She gave a little laugh at that and leaned into him, tilting her head up toward him.

"I'm sorry I didn't tell you how I felt sooner. And I know

you have another life, with responsibilities that you must see to. But if I can fit in there somewhere, I would be deliriously happy."

"Then prepare to be crazed out of your mind," he said, releasing her hands to allow his arms to come around her now. Despite the fact that her family stood nearby, he pulled her in close, touched his forehead to hers for a moment, and then found her lips. The kiss was too short and too chaste for Violet's liking, but it said what it needed to — that she was his and would be forever.

She wasn't sure how long they would have remained entwined together had they not heard a shout from just beyond them.

"Well, I *never!*"

Oh, yes, Linus. She had quite forgotten about him.

"First, my inn *burns* to the ground."

"I wouldn't say that, Linus," her father said in an attempt to placate him. "Why, much of it is still standing. Built of sturdy brick and stone, it was."

Linus shot him a hateful stare as the rest of the family, Violet and Owen included, looked on.

"And then, after my inn is burned to nothing even resembling a building any longer, I find my bride in the arms of another."

He turned his glare now onto the pair of them, and Violet could only look at him with pity, for he clearly lacked any love in his life. However, he would never have found it with her.

She began to rise and Owen, realizing just how unsteady she was, stood with her, holding her up.

"Linus," she said, catching his attention, and he stared at her with his arms crossed over his chest. "I am sorry that you have lost the inn, and I'm sorry that we will not be married. However, that was never to be the case. It was an... option, but one that didn't work out, for I love another."

Not that she would have married him anyway, for she knew now he would simply make her life miserable, but that wasn't something that she should share at the moment. He was angry enough as it was.

"Do you think that even matters?" he seethed. "We had a deal! You were promised to me!"

"That wasn't anything of which I was aware or agreed to," she said, and then turned back to look at what remained of the inn. Most of the fire had now settled into embers. The front half of the building was still somewhat intact. The back half — the family's quarters — was gone. Thankfully, the stables were untouched, as were the buildings on the other side.

She looked over at her father, and now that his attention was removed from Linus, she could see what a toll this was having on him. Everything he had ever owned was lost, burned down with the inn itself.

Her mother, normally the one whose emotions would be most apparent, stared on as though in a daze, unsure of what to do or even what to think. Daisy walked over to her now, placing an arm around her shoulders.

The sisters looked at one another, silent words passing between them. They would get through this — together. For that's what families did.

15

Violet sat on the small bed, staring out through the window at the countryside beyond. So much had happened over the past night and day that she should be exhausted, falling on the bed in a deep sleep, but it seemed it was far the opposite.

She didn't know what to do with herself. Normally when she couldn't sleep, as was often the case, she would light a candle and read long into the night, until her eyes closed of their own accord. But tonight, it was not to be. Her eyes were still gritty from smoke, her head still aching something fierce. She simply couldn't concentrate.

It was, of course, more than the physical symptoms. Violet's heart was both full of both love and agony.

Her childhood home, the building that had meant everything to her family, was in ashes. Her parents would be adrift, and as for her? Well, if Owen had meant everything he had said, then her entire world was about to change. Unless it had simply been an outcome of almost losing her, and now that he had time to consider the future, he thought differently.

A soft knock sounded at the door. Her family was staying at the inn of the nearby town, Reydon, for a couple of nights. Violet lifted a wrapper, borrowed from a neighbor in Southwold, around her shoulders before she crossed the room to open the door.

Her pulse quickened.

There stood Owen, leaning against the door in his signature slouch.

"I was hoping you were also awake."

"I am," she said, opening the door wider to allow him entrance. "You couldn't sleep either?"

He shook his head and stepped in.

"I suppose I probably shouldn't be here alone with you," he said, sending her a rueful smile.

"If anyone ever found out, then I would likely be ruined," she said with a shrug of one shoulder as she retreated a few steps, though she couldn't resist the small smile that escaped. "And then you'd have to marry me."

The words were out of her mouth before she even realized it, and she brought a hand to cover her lips. "I'm sorry, I didn't mean—"

He reached her in a few long strides.

"Would you, though?" he asked, his eyes desperately seeking hers. "Marry me, I mean?"

The trickle of hope that had been running through her became a stream.

"Oh, Owen, truly?" she gasped as his hands came to rest on her arms while her fingers curled into his shirt.

"Absolutely," he said firmly. "I realize this may not be the most romantic of proposals. Certainly not like any you would find in those stories you so love to read. I don't suppose any of them ever took place in an inn in Reydon?"

She laughed, shaking her head.

"Well, then this is the first. Would you marry me, Violet, even with all that it may mean for the two of us?"

"I would love nothing more," she murmured.

His arms came around her then, and no matter where she and Owen currently were or where they might end up, she decided that there was no other place she would rather be.

He kissed her, this time not quickly and not chastely, but with a possessive grip upon her lips. If she had ever doubted anything he might be saying, she no longer had any questions. For this was not the kiss of a man unsure of what he wanted. No, this was the kiss of a man determined.

For all that others might have thought her to be timid, she was no longer. Now that she had the man who loved her in front of her, whose love she returned in equal measure, she would take all that he had to offer.

"I promise," he said between kisses, as much as she willed him to continue them when he paused, "that I will do all in my power to stay with you, for the time between our reunions to be short, and to come home to you after each and every mission."

"You had better return home," she said, leaning back from him and looking deeply into his eyes. "Now that I have you, Owen, and know what love truly means, you had better not leave me."

"I won't," he said, placing his forehead against hers, brushing a soft kiss over her lips. "I promise I won't."

And with that, they clung to one another as though it was the last time they would be together. His hands brushed over her shoulders, along her arms, until they were running up and down her back, before encircling her waist possessively.

She leaned in to him until their bodies were flush

against one another, signaling that she wanted and needed more from him.

Violet slipped her hands inside the neck of his linen shirt, feeling his warm, hard chest beneath her fingertips.

When she reached to slip the bottom of his shirt from his trousers below, he stilled her fingers, but she looked up pleadingly at him.

"Love me, Owen?" she asked, and he seemed indecisive for a moment, but when she asked him once more, he nodded and kissed her again, his tongue sweeping into her mouth. His strong fingers came to the buttons of her dress, and he began to slip each one out of its hole.

How a man his size could be so gentle, Violet had no idea, but she was done with gentle. She helped him speed things along until there was nothing between them any longer.

He lifted her and carried her over to the bed, laying her down as though she were a priceless package. When he finally made love to her, it was more than any novel, any story ever could have prepared her for. More beautiful, more passionate, more desperate, and more perfect.

Afterward, she lay in his arms upon the small bed, the thin but clean blankets in tangles about them. She looked around her at the room, which she hadn't really assessed since their arrival, so dazed was she by all that had occurred.

This inn in Reydon, the neighboring town, reminded her much of the Wild Rose Inn. Clean, yet bare. Simple, and not overly tasteful. Decor that had been scavenged from different households, different eras, to attempt to trick the guest into thinking it had all been artfully arranged.

But it didn't matter. Not when she was with Owen.

A slight trickle of dread struck her as she stared at the ceiling. She had been a fool before in placing her affections with the wrong man. The fact she had given herself to Owen now—

But before the thought could even enter her mind, his strong, sure arm came around her, and she turned and looked into his eyes, which were as steady and unwavering as ever.

"What are you thinking about?" he asked, and her heart settled, knowing that if there was ever something she could trust in, it was him and all he had ever promised her.

"Of what is to come, I suppose," she said. "For us, for my family, for the inn."

"Well," he said, propping himself up on one elbow, which only highlighted the strength within his biceps muscle. "For us, I suppose marriage comes first, and as quickly as possible. Then, assuming we have time, we will return home together. I will see what the army has in store for me, and while I may have to hide you away with one of your sisters while I am gone, from there we begin our life together. How does that sound to you?"

"Wonderful," she said with a small smile, feeling a twinge of sadness. "Except the part where you leave."

"I know, love," he said, placing his index finger under her chin to tilt her head back up to him. "But I will always return."

She nodded, bending to kiss his finger.

"And as for your family, Iris and Westwood should hopefully be able to return home now, I would say, as it doesn't seem as though Comtois had any further communication with the French, considering he seemed to act alone. We shall hear news from the General soon regarding what knowledge of Westwood remains in France. Your parents have likely lost their inn for good, but between four noble sons-in-law, I am sure we can take care of them."

"Can you believe it?" Violet asked, shaking her head, "That all of us would marry so well? My father has likely never had a greater thrill in his life. Why, my parents will have nothing else to speak of when they meet someone new."

Owen chuckled at that.

"I'd best be going before someone discovers me," he said. "Though I'm sure Iris is already well aware of all that has gone on, however, that might be."

"Iris knows all," Violet said with a shrug, as she had come to accept the fact some time ago.

"Goodnight, Violet," Owen said after collecting his clothes and haphazardly dressing. He bent to place a kiss on her forehead.

"Goodnight, Owen," she said, the smile not leaving her face as he walked out of the room.

~

AND SO OWEN found himself two days later sitting with the three men who were married to the other Tavners sisters.

Once the initial business had been taken care of, they had all absconded to Dorchester's estate, which he and Marigold called home, a half day's ride from Southwold. Dorchester was actually surprisingly hospitable, and while Owen hadn't been opposed to the rooms at the Reydon inn, he couldn't say he didn't welcome the plush beds and servants eager to make their stay comfortable.

If he did have a request, it would have been to have the ability to stay with Violet, but they would still have a few weeks' wait until the banns could be read in Southwold's church, where the Tavners family were parishioners.

"Tavners has put himself in this situation," Dorchester

began after they had each taken a seat upon the chocolate-brown mahogany leather furniture in his library, brandies in hand. "If it wasn't for his daughters..."

"I understand that, truly I do," Greenwich said, leaning forward. "And all four of them have spent their lives working to manage that inn. Once they were old enough, I'm not sure the man lifted much of a finger."

"All he managed to do was lose all the money the family made," Dorchester said with a snort, and Westwood nodded in agreement.

"It was why he agreed to marry Violet off," Westwood said. "He could no longer afford to pay his debts. If he sold it, he could never have made enough to support himself and his wife for the rest of their lives."

"We cannot very well leave him to fend for himself," Owen finally said. "Look, I know I'm not a member of the family — yet — but they would be left with nothing."

"I don't think any of us would like to see that," Greenwich agreed. "But perhaps we make him sweat a bit? Wait a few days before letting him know what we've decided?"

"It's only fair," Westwood said with a grin, and Owen rubbed a hand against his beard.

"Whatever you think," he said. "But what is your plan?"

"He still owns the land the ruined inn sits upon," Greenwich said, twining his fingers together. "We could allow him to keep his manhood intact. We pay out his debt and buy the land from him, with the stipulation that he uses it to buy himself a cottage for him and his wife."

"And what do *we* do with the land?" Westwood asked, looking intrigued at what Greenwich had in mind.

"We rebuild the inn," Greenwich said with a smile. "We'd have to hire people to look after it, of course, to manage it and work there, but it could be an intriguing little business. We know four women who could provide plenty of advice. What do you think?"

"I don't mind the idea," said Dorchester with a shrug, "on one condition."

"The women agree," Owen finished for him with a bit of a laugh, and at that, they all chuckled before bringing their glasses together to celebrate the terms of their agreement.

~

"Fire," Violet said to Owen later that evening as they sat next to the hearth in matching chairs slightly distanced from her family, "is said to be cleansing. Meaning that, sometimes, it is what is needed for something new to grow in its place."

"Wise words," Owen responded as he took another sip of his drink.

It was rather odd, Violet thought, the lot of them sitting around doing nothing but drinking tea and brandy, and eating pastries and all manner of delightful meals. They had spent their entire lives in motion, doing one thing or another, and all of this sitting was beginning to grate on Violet. She wondered if it bothered her sisters in the same way.

"It does," Daisy had said when she asked as much, "but I have learned how, for the most part, to keep myself busy. Vi, it will soon be the same for you."

"It is rather odd to consider such a thing," Violet said now, and Owen looked at her questioningly.

"I was just thinking that soon I will have nothing to do," she explained, and he chuckled.

"Not to worry, there is always much to entertain oneself with," he said. "I am not one to be idle either. And now,

Violet, your days will be full of work — or leisure — of your own choosing, and no one else's."

She smiled and looked down at her lap where a book rested, waiting for her to pick it up. She looked forward to it — she had already scoured Lord Dorchester's extensive library — but for now, she was content in conversing with the man who would soon be her husband.

"It's rather odd," she said, "that I hardly knew you but a short time ago, and now we are to be married." She laughed, soft and low. "And to think that I never thought it would be possible for me. That I would have married Linus, with the idea that that's all there would ever be for me."

"Then thank goodness I came along," Owen said with a grin, and Violet smiled back, though she was all serious now.

"Thank goodness you did."

"I love you, Violet."

"And I you, Owen."

When they joined hands, Violet knew she would never let go.

EPILOGUE

July, 1818

"Can you believe it?" Daisy asked, her voice just above a whisper. "It is almost surreal."

They stood on the sand in front of the newly built Wild Rose Inn as the waves lapped the shore behind them. Violet figured they must have created quite a picture, the four of them, now ladies dressed in their finery, standing in a line looking up at the newly refinished brick building.

It retained a similar feel to the original, but now incorporated the styles of the day. Their husbands had wasted no time in rebuilding the inn, and while they had not been frugal about it, they also had been sensible. They were building an inn on the seaside, not a noble estate.

"It's rather amazing, isn't it?" Iris asked. "Here we are, ladies each and every one of us, and yet we are back where we started — the inn where we worked ourselves ragged."

"I think that might be a bit of an exaggeration, Iris," Marigold said, but Iris shook her head to silence her.

"I do miss it sometimes," Violet said softly, and they all

turned to look at her in surprise. "The place, not the work. Do you not?" she asked. "We had so many memories in our original inn. No matter where we are now, this is where we came from."

"That's true," Daisy said with a nod. "The inn made us who we are."

They shared a smile then and hooked their hands together as they walked toward the doors that led to a spacious courtyard that overlooked the sea beyond.

It was beautiful, and the hope was to attract visitors looking to spend some time near the sea.

"Ladies," the Duke of Greenwich said as he held the door open for them. "Looking lovely, as always." He stooped to place a kiss on Daisy's nose, and she smiled up prettily at him.

"It is lovely in here," Marigold said as she looked around the guests' sitting room, which now overlooked the ocean instead of the road behind. "I shan't want to leave."

"Well, leave you must," Owen said, entering the room. "For I expect this place will soon be full of guests looking to enjoy all that beautiful Southwold has to offer."

"Run by the most experienced innkeepers in the business," Elias Tavners said, joining them and raising a glass.

Violet smiled as she looked around at her family, together once more. Since the fire, her father had, surprisingly, been somewhat responsible with the income he earned, for now, he knew it was limited. He was living off of the benevolence of his sons-in-law, who owned the inn he now managed, at least for the time being.

"Come, my lady," Owen said to her, holding out a hand, "Let me show you the greatest view in all of Southwold."

Violet gladly took it as Owen led her over to the beautiful Venetian window overlooking the sea below.

"Are you happy?" he asked her, and she nodded.

"Very much so. I'm not sure that there is a woman in England who is happier to have this war with Napoleon over."

He chuckled. "I'm sure there are many who share your sentiments. And many who are less fortunate than we are."

Violet was silent for a moment as she considered the sober thought. She knew how lucky she was to have her husband returned home to her. Many women would never see their men again, lost to the horrors of war. There had been some long days and nights when she found herself sitting at the window, watching the road below as she waited for Owen to return, fear in her heart each and every time he was out on assignment.

He looked over at her now, accurately assessing her thoughts.

"I made you a promise," he reminded her, placing a hand on her arm before slowly drawing her toward him. "I told you I would return home to you. And here we are."

"Here we are," she said, practically breathless as tears threatened.

"Don't cry," he whispered as he cupped her face and lowered his lips to hers. "For I've got you, Violet. Now and always."

∽

THE END

∽

Dear reader,

I hope you have enjoyed reading the stories of the Tavners sisters as much as I loved writing them!

These books will always have a special place in my heart, as I wrote them just before and after the birth of my second son. While these are, of course, love stories, they also tell the story of the bond between sisters. I have two sisters of my own and they are two of the very closest people to me.

If you enjoyed The Blooming Brides, I would love for you to meet the women of my Bluestocking Scandals! You can find a preview of the first book in the pages after this one, or you can go right to the book page of <u>Designs on a Duke.</u>

If you haven't yet signed up for my newsletter, I would love to have you join us! You will also receive links to giveaways, sales, new releases, and learn all about my coffee addiction, my struggle to keep my plants alive, and how much trouble one loveable wolf-lookalike dog can get into. <u>www.elliestclair.com/ellies-newsletter</u>

Or you can join my Facebook group, Ellie St. Clair's Ever Afters, and stay in touch daily.

Until next time, happy reading!
With love,
Ellie

$\sim$

Designs on a Duke
The Bluestocking Scandals Book 1

HER SECRET WILL SAVE A LEGACY. **But it could also break her heart when faced with a duke caught between two identities.**

The daughter of a famed architect, Rebecca Lambert has been raised among the nobility yet understands the circumstances of her birth. Becoming an architect is a dream, not an option, until she must assume an identity to protect her father's name.

No one was pleased when Valentine St. Vincent was shockingly named the Duke of Wyndham -- least of all Valentine himself. He has always led with his fists, but now he must become the man his brother was supposed to be.

When Valentine hires Rebecca's father, she takes on the work herself. But as she spends more and more time at the duke's homes, she finds herself hopelessly falling for a man she can never have. For the Duke of Wyndham must marry a woman for her dowry and respectability -- two things Rebecca can never provide.

Will Rebecca and Val resign themselves to the lives chosen for them, or those they were born to live?

～

AN EXCERPT FROM DESIGNS ON
A DUKE

A *sneak peek...*
  Valentine St. Vincent, the sixth Duke of
  Wyndham, was tired.

He was tired of balls. He was tired of operas. He was
tired of pretending to be the Duke of Wyndham when all he
had ever aspired to be was a man making a name for
himself in his chosen profession, which was the only thing
he truly excelled at. One who would be perfectly happy
spending his life without any pressure or great responsi-
bility placed upon him.

But then his brother had died. His father had died. His
cousin was deemed illegitimate. And then the old duke had
finally succumbed to the illness that had kept him
bedridden for years, and Val remained the fortuitous one to
be alive and declared the duke after a lengthy inquiry by the
College of Arms.

He let himself into his house — though it was styled
more of a mansion than anything else, and finding his
butler utterly absent, he hung his hat up himself.

A crash resounded from down the hall and he smiled to

himself. Jemima. At least some things never changed. His sister was still as curious in unraveling the next great scientific discovery. He didn't understand half of it, though she was always more than pleased to provide a running commentary of her most recent hypothesis. Currently, it was something to do with the effects of the cleanliness — or lack thereof — of water.

He strode through the foyer to what was supposed to be a ballroom but had become Jemima's laboratory. He found her blonde head bent over a microscope, so focused that she didn't even look up when he walked into the room.

"Good to see you haven't destroyed our new home quite yet," he said, and she yelped as she jumped up.

"Val! You scared me."

He chuckled as he tapped a hand against his leg, where an old injury still aggravated him from time to time.

"Where is everyone?"

"Hmm?"

Her mind was still elsewhere.

"Dexter wasn't at the door. Usually he is so eager to prove himself as a new butler that I can hardly untie my own cloak."

"Dexter? Oh yes, he came through here not long ago."

"Jem?" He tried not to sigh in exasperation, but he only needed a moment of her time.

"Right. Ummm, he had some people with him. I think they went into the parlor. So did Mother."

She waved her hand toward the end of the room, where the parlor was located.

"People? Oh, right — the architect." He slapped a hand to his forehead. "I completely forgot."

"And you call me absentminded."

When she finally looked up at him, her eyes widened and she snorted.

"You certainly cannot greet them looking like that."

"Why not?"

"You look as though someone just gave you a sound pummeling."

"I actually came out the victor, thank you very much."

He looked down at himself and saw that his sister had a point.

She was shaking her head now.

"I really don't understand why you continue to go back to Jackson's."

He walked over to the table and tweaked her nose as though she was still a girl and not a woman over twenty.

"And I don't understand why you enjoy mixing your liquids in here all day, but I leave you be, don't I?"

"Fair point."

"Very well. I best wash up and then I'll meet with the architect. Though I wish Mother hadn't pressured me into hiring one. We have no money to pay for him."

"That's why you're supposed to marry someone wealthy," Jemima said absently, returning to her work, apparently dismissing him.

Val sighed as he found the stairs and began to trudge up to his room. Truth be told, the only joy he could find in his current life was through some physical activity and boxing served the dual purpose of keeping up his strength as well as releasing the tension that seemed to build as he sat at his damned desk all day working in the ledgers the old duke had left. Val had fired his man of business who had supposedly handled everything but truly bungled it all. Val was determined to figure this out on his own before he trusted another to look after things for him.

He entered the large ducal suite, aware that it was too depressing, too dismal. It made him feel as though he was living in some remote Scottish castle. He'd have the architect take a look at this room, see if there was anything to be done.

Although his sister had said that *architects* had arrived — he only recalled asking one to come to consult with him. He certainly couldn't afford two. Hopefully the man had simply brought an assistant.

He stripped off his bloody shirt and threw it on the bed, realizing as he did so that he had forgotten to call for the valet, and Dexter wouldn't know to tell Archie he had returned. Well, soon enough, word would get round that he was home and Archie would be through the bedroom door and ready to offer him his assistance as well as his commentary.

He was not the most conventional of servants, but he was one of the few not constantly awaiting his every command, which was beginning to unnerve him.

Well, until Archie arrived, he supposed he could select his own clothes.

He opened the door to his dressing room, reaching out a hand as he did — and touched something very soft, very silky, and very smooth.

"Who's there?" he demanded, opening the door wider to allow more light in.

There stood a woman, her greenish-brown eyes wide as they stared at him over a pert nose. Her jet black hair was pulled back from her head, seemingly long and straight as pieces tumbled down from the pins over her back. What he couldn't tear his eyes away from? Those cherry-red lips, just begging to be kissed. They parted now, as though she was about to say something, but just then he heard a sound from the corridor.

"Your grace?"

Not Archie. Dexter.

For a moment, Val forgot that he was a duke, that he had no one to answer to but himself. He went back to being a young man, who was frightened of his father discovering any transgression. Before he could even think of what he was doing, he stepped into the dressing room, nearly pressing himself against the woman, and shut the door behind him.

∼

REBECCA STOOD SO STILL in shock that she had no idea what she was supposed to do next. She was an intelligent woman. She should have a witty response on the tip of her tongue.

But inspiration had never come quickly to her. Rather, she had to stew on something, turn it over in her mind until just the right thought entered and answered her current problem.

"Ah... you must be the Duke of Wyndham," she finally managed before sensing movement. "Did you just nod?"

"I did," he said, his voice deeper, rougher than she had expected. "My apologies. Rather idiotic of me. Yes, I am the Duke of Wyndham."

"Well, I cannot say this is how I thought I would make your acquaintance."

"Rather silly for us to be hiding in here," he said with the slightest of chuckles. "I, ah, saw a beautiful woman, heard a voice in the hall, and acted on instinct."

"To hide with a woman?" she asked, pleased that he couldn't see the flush in her cheeks at being called beautiful.

"Err..."

"You don't need to answer that," she said quickly. What had gotten into her?

But then he laughed. His laugh was a low rumble that began deep in his chest before resounding throughout the dressing chamber. It was one of those laughs that was so contagious, one had no choice but to join in.

And so she did. It was freeing, chasing away both the awkwardness for a moment and the need for either of them to say anything within this strange encounter.

"I think he's gone now," the duke said after their laughter subsided, and sure enough, the sounds of his butler calling out "Your grace?" was no longer. "Poor Dexter. He will be most distressed. At least he likely found my shirt to take to the valet for laundering. That should keep him busy for a time."

"Your shirt?"

"Yes, it had some... stains."

"I see."

Rebecca was quite confused by this entire encounter, but who was she to question a duke?

"I, ah, best be going now," she said, slowly inching around him, doing all she could to not slide her body over his as she sought the door. Relief swept over her when she found the handle, and she turned the knob open, allowing light to enter once more though she didn't look back. "I shall see you in the parlor," she managed, before slipping out the door and nearly running out of the bedroom, along the corridor, and down the stairs.

～

VALENTINE STOOD THERE IN SHOCK, staring after the beauty. One look at her and he had turned into a blithering fool.

It was this entire new situation, he told himself. He was having a difficult time learning how he was supposed to interact with his peers, his servants, and... whoever this woman was. As she had escaped his room so quickly that he nearly wondered if she had seen a mouse, he realized that he had no idea who she was or what she was doing in his bedchamber. Apparently not a gift, he realized with a rueful laugh.

He was right in that his soiled shirt had been taken away, but he knew it would take him a great deal longer to dress himself than with the help of his valet. With company about he was expected, as a duke, to always be fully dressed in a waistcoat and cravat, as uncomfortable as they were. He walked to the door, throwing it open.

"Archie!" he bellowed, but instead of seeing his valet approach, a tall, distinguished gentleman he had never seen before was wandering down his corridor. What in the...

"Hello, sir," the man said, "to what do I owe the pleasure?"

"Ah... I'm not entirely sure," Val said, scratching his hair, which had been cut fairly short upon his arrival in London. He missed his usual longer locks. "Just who are you?"

"Why, I am Albert Lambert, of course."

"Lambert — the architect. Right," Val said, frowning. What kind of architect had he hired? "I thought you were awaiting me in the parlor."

"The parlor? We finished the parlor weeks ago!" Lambert said, further confusing Val. "We must now continue with the ballroom."

"That will be the last of it," Val said. "We must make sure we build my sister a proper laboratory first."

"Laboratory?" the man repeated back to him, a frown marring his face. "I wasn't told of a laboratory."

"Yes, well, I will explain everything when we discuss the project further," Val said, relieved when he saw Archie approaching down the hall. "I will be down to meet with you shortly, Mr. Lambert. My apologies for my tardiness."

He stepped back into the room, Archie following him with a questioning look, as Mr. Lambert nodded and strode away in the other direction.

My, but this was a strange day.

~

KEEP READING <u>DESIGNS ON A DUKE</u>*!*

ALSO BY ELLIE ST. CLAIR

The Unconventional Ladies Box Set

To the Time of the Highlanders

A Time to Wed

A Time to Love

A Time to Dream

Thieves of Desire

The Art of Stealing a Duke's Heart

A Jewel for the Taking

A Prize Worth Fighting For

Gambling for the Lost Lord's Love

Romance of a Robbery

Thieves of Desire Box Set

The Bluestocking Scandals

Designs on a Duke

Inventing the Viscount

Discovering the Baron

The Valet Experiment

Writing the Rake

Risking the Detective

A Noble Excavation

A Gentleman of Mystery

The Bluestocking Scandals Box Set: Books 1-4

The Bluestocking Scandals Box Set: Books 5-8

Happily Ever After

The Duke She Wished For

Someday Her Duke Will Come

Once Upon a Duke's Dream

He's a Duke, But I Love Him

Loved by the Viscount

Because the Earl Loved Me

Happily Ever After Box Set Books 1-3

Happily Ever After Box Set Books 4-6

The Victorian Highlanders

Duncan's Christmas - (prequel)

<u>Callum's Vow</u>

<u>Finlay's Duty</u>

<u>Adam's Call</u>

<u>Roderick's Purpose</u>

<u>Peggy's Love</u>

<u>The Victorian Highlanders Box Set Books 1-5</u>

Searching Hearts

Duke of Christmas (prequel)

Quest of Honor

Clue of Affection

Hearts of Trust

Hope of Romance

Promise of Redemption

Searching Hearts Box Set (Books 1-5)

Christmas

Christmastide with His Countess

Her Christmas Wish

Merry Misrule

A Match Made at Christmas

A Match Made in Winter

Standalones

Always Your Love

The Stormswept Stowaway

A Touch of Temptation

For a full list of all of Ellie's books, please see

www.elliestclair.com/books.

ABOUT THE AUTHOR

Ellie has always loved reading, writing, and history. For many years she has written short stories, non-fiction, and has worked on her true love and passion -- romance novels.

In every era there is the chance for romance, and Ellie enjoys exploring many different time periods, cultures, and geographic locations. No matter when or where, love can always prevail. She has a particular soft spot for the bad boys of history, and loves a strong heroine in her stories.

Ellie and her husband love nothing more than spending time at home with their children and Husky cross. Ellie can typically be found at the lake in the summer, pushing the stroller all year round, and, of course, with her computer in her lap or a book in hand.

She also loves corresponding with readers, so be sure to contact her!

www.elliestclair.com
ellie@elliestclair.com

Printed in Great Britain
by Amazon